animal planet

AWESOME ADVENTURES

Silver Dolphin

Silver Dolphin Books
An imprint of Printers Row Publishing Group
A division of Readerlink Distribution Services, LLC
9717 Pacific Heights Blvd, San Diego, CA 92121
www.silverdolphinbooks.com

Printers Row Publishing Group is a division of Readerlink Distribution Services, LLC.
Silver Dolphin Books is a registered trademark of Readerlink Distribution Services, LLC.

All notations of errors or omissions should be addressed to Silver Dolphin Books, Editorial Department, at the
above address.

ISBN: 978-1-64517-836-1
Manufactured, printed, and assembled in Heshan, China.
First printing, June 2021. LP/06/21
25 24 23 22 21 1 2 3 4 5

Picture Credits:

Dolphin Rescue: All images © iStock unless otherwise noted; Cover: © Stephen Frink; © NOAA: pp. 76-77
background and inset, p. 86 blue whale

Puppy Rescue Riddle: All images © iStock

Farm Friends Escape!: All images © iStock unless otherwise noted;
Cover: © John M Lund Photography Inc

Contents

animal planet™

Dolphin Rescue

Catherine Nichols
Illustrated by Bryan Langdo

Contents

HELLO!

Dolphins are curious. They often pop out of the water to see what's going on.

CHAPTER 1

A Terrible Mess

Bang! *Bang! Bang!*

"Yikes!" Atticus spilled the milk he was pouring over his cornflakes. "Who's pounding on the door so early?"

"I'll go and find out," Maddie said. She handed her brother a napkin. Then she hurried to the door.

Mrs. Grady, their next-door neighbor, didn't wait to be invited. She rushed into the Cardozo family's house. "It's a mess!" she cried out. "A complete mess!"

"What's a mess, Mrs. Grady?" asked Mr. Cardozo. Maddie and Atticus's father stepped into the kitchen. He was wearing his bright-orange jacket and rubber boots. Maddie and Atticus knew this meant he was off to his boat. Their father trapped lobsters for a living.

Mrs. Grady placed her hands on her hips. "Someone has dumped trash all over my lawn."

Maddie and Atticus ran to the door to look. Sure enough, Mrs. Grady's lawn was covered with empty milk and juice cartons, egg shells, bottle caps, and paper towels.

"It's my own garbage!" she moaned. "Who would do such a thing?"

"Don't worry, Mrs. Grady. Maddie and

• SHORE THING •

The area where land meets the ocean is the coast. The towns there are coastal towns. Why do people like to live in coastal towns? Some like to be near the beach. Some have jobs on the ocean, such as fishing. Some work in restaurants, hotels, and shops for tourists who visit the beach.

Marine Fact

OCEAN BOUNTY

When people visit a coastal town, they may enjoy a lobster dinner fresh from the ocean waters.

Atticus will clean up that mess in no time," Mr. Cardozo said.

Atticus opened his mouth to protest. He closed it when he saw his father's face.

"Right away, Dad," Maddie said. She tugged her nine-year-old brother's arm. "Come on, Atticus. Let's hurry so we can get to the aquarium on time."

Maddie was a junior volunteer at the Lymesport Aquarium of Maine. Since joining the team of volunteers on her tenth birthday, she had touched a sea urchin and cleaned out the octopus tank. She had fed a seal and helped paint a wall mural. Today was the launch of the aquarium's latest project: "Save Sea Animals—Keep Our Beaches Clean." Maddie had promised to come in early.

She wanted to help get things ready for the big day. Atticus was tagging along.

Working together, Maddie and Atticus bagged up the trash on Mrs. Grady's lawn.

"Yuck!" Atticus exclaimed, holding some sticky wrappers between two fingers. "Mrs. Grady must have a sweet tooth."

Maddie stopped to wipe the sweat off her damp forehead. Although it was only nine on a Saturday morning, the July day was already hot. "I wonder who made this mess," she said. "This is such a friendly town. I can't picture any of our neighbors doing anything so mean. Can you?"

Atticus shrugged. "You never know. Maybe someone doesn't like Mrs. Grady and is getting revenge." Atticus read a *lot* of mystery stories.

WHO LIVES ON OR NEAR THE BEACH?

Many animals live at the edge of the water. They can find food in the ocean. Rocks, cliffs, and sand provide shelter for animals.

PELICANS come to the coasts in the summer to have their babies. Both parents fish and bring food for the chicks.

SEA TURTLES live in the ocean. They come onto the beach to dig a nest in the sand and lay their eggs. When the babies hatch, they flop down the beach to get to the water.

HERMIT CRABS don't have shells of their own. They climb into shells that other animals have left behind.

SEAGULLS are excellent fliers. They grab scraps of food from fishing boats. They steal fish from other birds. They even grab bits of food thrown into the air by humans.

HORSESHOE CRABS have long tails they use to flip over if they end up on their backs.

RED FOXES dig dens in sand dunes, the mountains of sand at the beach.

The **OSPREY** lives in trees near the coast and eats fish.

"Like who?"

Atticus scrunched his nose as he thought. "Like one of her students, someone she failed." Mrs. Grady taught third grade. Atticus had been in her class the year before, and she had given him a B in Handwriting. Until then Atticus had been a straight A student.

Maddie laughed. "Was it *you*?" she kidded.

"You know it couldn't have been me," he replied seriously. "We were together all morning."

◢ ◢ ◢

Inside the house, Mrs. Grady was sipping tea. She seemed calmer.

"All done," Atticus said. He went to

the sink and scrubbed his hands. "You have sticky garbage," he complained.

Mrs. Grady laughed. "Thank you both," she said. "Did I hear you say you're going to the aquarium?"

Their father glanced at his watch. "I'm afraid I can't take you guys. I'm already late. I need to get to the boat."

"That's okay, Dad," Maddie said.

"We'll take the bus," Atticus added.

Thomas Cardozo was a single parent. He worked long hours and took care of the kids by himself. That didn't leave a lot of time for rides to the aquarium. Maddie and Atticus had a lot of practice getting around without him.

"I can take you to the aquarium if you'd like," Mrs. Grady offered. "I have to go in that direction anyway."

"That's great!" Maddie exclaimed.

"Yes, thank you," said Mr. Cardozo. "That would be a big help."

Just then a crash came from overhead. It was followed by a yelp of pain.

Mrs. Grady jumped. "What was that?"

"That," said Mr. Cardozo, "is my nephew Zach."

"He probably fell out of my top bunk," Atticus said. "Again."

◢ ◢ ◢

Splash!

Atall, skinny teenage boy appeared in the kitchen doorway. He yawned. At his heels was a large, shaggy dog.

"This is Zach Quintos," Mr. Cardozo said to Mrs. Grady. "He's staying with us for the summer." He pointed to the dog slumped at Zach's feet. "And this hairy creature is Norville, Zach's dog. Zach, this is Mrs. Grady, our next-door neighbor."

Zach mumbled his hello. He dumped half a box of cornflakes into his bowl.

"Nice to meet you, Zach," said Mrs. Grady. "I'm taking Maddie and Atticus to the aquarium. Would you care to come along?"

Zach crunched and swallowed a big mouthful of cereal before answering. "No, thanks. I have big plans for today."

"What could possibly be better than a trip to the aquarium?" Maddie asked.

"I'm spending the morning on the beach," Zach said.

"Going swimming?" Atticus asked.

Zach shook his head. "I never learned how. I can dog paddle a little, and that's it."

"How come you never learned?" Maddie asked. Everyone she knew had learned to swim before they could tie their shoes.

Zach shrugged. "I don't know. I guess I just never needed to know how. We don't do a lot of swimming in the city."

"You should take lessons," Maddie said.

"That's a great idea, Maddie," said Mr. Cardozo as he reached down to grab Norville by the collar. He pulled the dog away from the kitchen rug he was chewing. "This dog of yours isn't trained," he told his nephew. "Yesterday he broke the screen door to the backyard. He could use a few obedience lessons."

"Norville?" Zach looked surprised. "He's still young. He'll grow out of it."

After breakfast, Mrs. Grady drove Maddie and Atticus to the aquarium. It was all the way at the other end of the island, about a twenty minute drive.

SEA GLASS

At an aquarium, you can see all kinds of ocean animals and plants. You can learn about the places they live, what they eat, and how they survive.

Scientists at many aquariums study the animals that live in the ocean. They learn as much as they can about ocean animals, so they will know how to help them—in their ocean homes and at the aquarium.

Marine Fact

GO FISH

Aquariums can be large enough to hold a whale shark or small enough for a tiny goldfish.

Looking out the car window, Maddie thought how lucky she was to live where she did. Surrounded by water, the small island could only be reached by a bridge. Everyone who lived there knew and looked out for one another. Maddie sniffed the salty sea air and smiled. They were almost at the aquarium.

A minute later, Mrs. Grady pulled up in front of the bright-white building. Before she drove off, she thanked Maddie and Atticus once more for their help with the trash. "I just hope it doesn't happen again," she said.

⚓ ⚓ ⚓

Inside the aquarium, right by the visitor center, was the mural Maddie had helped paint.

"Can you guess which part I worked on?" she asked her brother.

"Let me see." Atticus pretended to examine the mural. Then he pointed to a pod of dolphins frolicking in the ocean.

"How did you guess?"

"That's all you ever draw, read, or talk about: dolphins, dolphins, dolphins."

"That's because they're fascinating," Maddie said. "Dolphins are mammals, not fish, you know."

"Yes, I *do* know," said Atticus. "You've told me exactly forty-two times now."

A man wearing a bow tie was standing behind the counter at the visitor center. "Maddie, I'm glad you're here!" he exclaimed. "I have something for you." He handed her a small box.

"What is it?" Maddie asked.

Inside the box was a real shark tooth on a shiny silver chain.

"That's a thank-you present for your hard work," Mr. Marshall said. "All our volunteers get one after they have been with us for one year."

"Thank you!" Maddie said. "I'll wear it always." She slipped on the necklace.

"And don't forget Cleanup Day is next week," Mr. Marshall reminded her. "We're hoping to pick up every piece of garbage on the beach."

"We wouldn't miss it for anything," Maddie assured him. "We know how important it is to keep trash away from sea animals."

"More cleaning," Atticus groaned after Mr. Marshall had left. "Didn't we do enough of that this morning?"

"It's for a good cause. You're going!" Maddie told her frowning brother. "Now I have to get to work. The 'Save Sea Animals' exhibit opens in a few hours."

CLEANING CREW

Many coastal towns set aside a special day to clean up beach areas. People pick up all the trash on the shore. They clean up the areas around the rivers and streams that flow into the ocean.

DO TOUCH!

At the touch pool, you can see and even touch some tide pool animals.

Marine Fact

HANDLE WITH CARE

If you are allowed to pick up an animal, hold it gently in your hands.

Animals that live in tide pools need skills to survive when the tide goes out. Some, such as barnacles, grip tightly to rocks so they aren't washed away. Others, such as sea slugs, hide under seaweed to stay wet until the tide comes back in.

That afternoon, Maddie and Atticus took the bus home. Their cottage was just a few short blocks from the marina where their dad kept his boat. They decided to get off at the marina in case their dad's boat came in early.

Atticus ran ahead when they reached the marina. He liked to see the seagulls looking for fish scraps on the pier. He watched with delight as two seagulls fought for a piece of fish. Then he saw what they were really fighting over. The trash bin at the end of the pier was on its side. Half-eaten sandwiches, chicken bones, and plastic cups were strewn over the wood boards.

"It happened again!" he called to his sister.

Maddie came running. When she reached the spilled trash, she stopped and stared. "Twice in one day," she gasped. "Is that an accident?"

Atticus shook his head. "I doubt it."

"We'd better clean up." Maddie crouched to pick up a cup. "If this stuff gets in the ocean, it will harm the animals."

For once Atticus didn't argue. He got to work helping his sister pick up the trash.

When they finished, Atticus straightened up and pointed to a figure coming toward them. "There's Zach," he said. "He must be coming back from the beach."

Zach waved to them as he got closer, and they waved back. He ambled over to where Maddie and Atticus were standing, a towel around his neck.

"How was the beach?" Maddie asked.

Before Zach could answer, a furry blur raced toward them. Zach, facing the ocean, couldn't see Norville bounding up to him.

Atticus yelled, "Watch out!" But it was too late. Norville was excited to see his owner. He crashed into Zach.

"Whoa!" Zach yelled as he teetered at the edge of the pier. He lost his balance, and with a huge splash, he fell into the water. His head bobbed up once, and then it sank below the surface.

⊿ ⊿ ⊿

A Sea Rescue

Maddie and Atticus stood frozen over the edge of the pier. Norville whimpered softly. Another second ticked away before Maddie sprang into action. "Help!" she yelled. "Help!" But the dock was deserted in the early part of the afternoon. All the boaters were out on the water.

Then Zach's head bobbed up to the surface. He gasped for air. His arms paddled the water.

"What do we do?" Atticus tugged on his sister's arm.

"I'll have to try and save him." She kicked off her sandals and prepared to jump.

"No," Atticus said, pulling her back. "You're not a lifeguard."

Zach sank again.

"We can't let him drown!" Maddie cried.

Atticus didn't respond; he was staring at the water. "Look!" He pointed to a silver shape in the ocean.

A fin appeared. It was swimming toward them. When it got near the pier, it dove. Right before Maddie's and Atticus's eyes, Zach popped out of the water.

Maddie shouted, "It's a dolphin! It's helping Zach."

Sure enough, the dolphin was pushing Zach toward the shore. Its broad body pressed against the boy's back as they glided forward.

"What's it doing?" Atticus asked.

"It's pushing Zach to shallow water," Maddie said.

The dolphin stopped before it reached the shore. Zach tumbled back into the water.

"Stand up!" Atticus called out, running to Zach. "The water isn't deep."

Zach scrambled to his feet. He waded the rest of the way to dry land. The dolphin remained nearby, its sleek head bobbing in the water. Once Zach had reached land, the dolphin gave a chirp and swam away.

Maddie waved goodbye. Then she ran down to meet the boys. Zach was now sprawled on the sand. Norville, barking wildly, threw himself on top of Zach and began licking his salty face.

Zach opened his eyes and sat up.

CURIOUS AS A DOLPHIN

Dolphins are very curious about everything, including people. Sometimes dolphins will surround a boat and swim alongside it. The dolphins may leap out of the water all around the boat. Scientists think they might be leaping to get a better look.

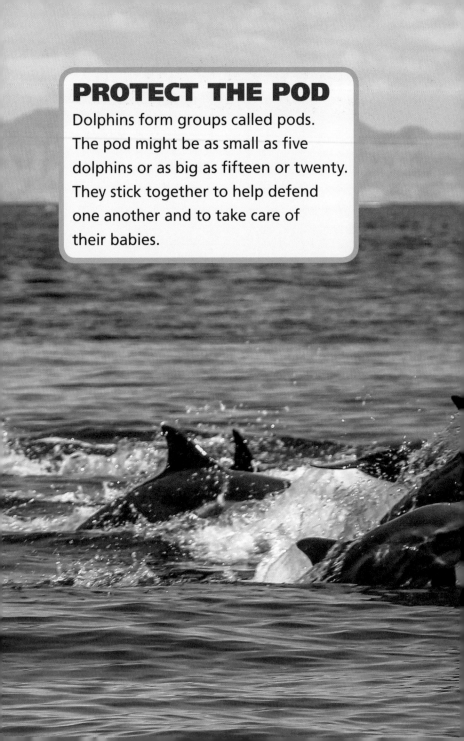

PROTECT THE POD

Dolphins form groups called pods. The pod might be as small as five dolphins or as big as fifteen or twenty. They stick together to help defend one another and to take care of their babies.

Marine Fact

ME TOO!

Gannets fly overhead when dolphin pods circle a school of fish. The birds dive under the water to grab fish before the dolphins eat them all.

Average swimming speed for these dolphins is about 7 miles per hour. They can zoom up to 20 miles per hour for short distances.

Zach spit out some water. He coughed and took a deep breath. "You know," he said, "Uncle Thomas might be right. Norville probably *could* use some training."

▲ ▲ ▲

The Mystery of the Dumped Trash

When their dad got home later that afternoon, Atticus met him at the door.

"Zach fell off the pier and almost drowned," Atticus told his father.

"Then a dolphin came and pushed Zach to shore," Maddie added. "I'm pretty sure it was an Atlantic white-sided dolphin. It was unbelievably cool."

"Wow." Mr. Cardozo shook his head.

"That's amazing! Zach could have been in serious trouble." He looked thoughtful for a moment. "Where is he?"

"He went straight to bed after he dried off," Atticus answered. "He said he was exhausted."

"Well, wake him. We need to take him to the doctor and get him checked out," said Mr. Cardozo. "What were you kids doing at the dock in the first place?"

Maddie and Atticus explained about the spilled trash.

Their father frowned. "Hmm. That's not good. I was telling some of our neighbors about Mrs. Grady's trash problem. They said the same thing had happened to them. Mr. Barone found trash on his lawn on Thursday. And the

Greenbergs on Friday."

"It's a mystery." Atticus's eyes sparkled.

"Yes, one that's stinking up our neighborhood," said his sister.

⚓ ⚓ ⚓

Maddie and Atticus woke early Sunday morning. They decided to let their father sleep in. They made their own breakfast. Maddie got the eggs from the fridge while Atticus went to get the newspaper. He opened the front door. Then he stopped suddenly and called out, "Maddie, you'd better come here!"

His sister hurried over and gasped. Both trash bins were on their sides. Piles of trash spilled out of them and all across the lawn. Maddie spotted yesterday's pizza crusts among the trash. "I can't believe it," she said.

"Believe it," Atticus said. "You're not dreaming." To prove it, he pinched her arm.

"Ouch! Stop that." She stamped her foot. "This is serious. We have to get this mess cleaned up before Dad wakes up."

"Don't touch it yet," Atticus ordered. He ran back inside the house. He returned with their father's camera. He snapped photos of the trash. "This is evidence," he said.

TAKE NOTE

How do you solve a mystery?

1. Observe: To figure out what happened, look for clues.

2. Investigate: Look around for evidence— for example, footprints may tell you whether someone was wearing sneakers, work boots, or had bare feet. Ask people what they saw.

3. Take notes: Write down the details. When did it happen? Who was there? What else was going on?

4. Consider the evidence: Is there more than one possible conclusion? Be logical—consider how likely or unlikely something is.

"You're acting crazy," Maddie said.

"Yesterday I called this a mystery," Atticus said. "I was only joking then, but it *is* a mystery, a real one. Who's doing this? And why?"

Maddie nodded. "You're right. These can't be accidents. Something fishy is going on. We have to figure it out before Saturday."

"Why then?"

"That's the aquarium's big beach Cleanup Day." Maddie straightened the chain of her shark-tooth necklace. "How can we tell people to keep the beaches clean if we can't keep our own street clean?"

"Maybe that's the reason the Trasher is doing this," Atticus said.

"I need to write all this down."

Maddie nodded. "Yes, but first we have to pick up this mess."

⬧ ⬧ ⬧

After the trash was bagged and back in the bins, Maddie and Atticus went inside. Their father was at the stove, frying eggs. "What were you two doing out so early?" he asked.

"The Trasher struck again," Maddie said.

"This time it was *our* trash!" Atticus added, going to wash his hands.

"This is getting serious," Dad said. "Maybe we should call the police."

"The police have more important

SOLVE IT!

If you want to solve a mystery, it helps to have a mystery-solving kit. This should include a notebook, pen or pencil, bags (to carry evidence), and a camera. Binoculars are helpful, too—they help you see things that are far away.

crimes to take care of," Maddie said.

"Besides," Atticus said, "you don't have to worry. Maddie and I are on the case. We'll track down the Trasher."

"I feel better already," said Dad. "Now eat your breakfast. Where's your cousin?"

Atticus shrugged. "Knowing him, probably asleep."

◢ ◢ ◢

After breakfast, Atticus took a notebook and wrote "Casebook" in big letters on the cover. Inside, he jotted down the names of the people who had had trash spilled on their lawns and the dates when it had happened. He showed his list to Maddie. "Did I get them all?"

Maddie nodded. "Yes, you got all the people. But what about the trash by the dock?"

"Good point!" Atticus scribbled some more. "There. All done. Now what?"

Thursday, July 21
Mr. Barone

Friday, July 22
The Greenbergs

Saturday, July 23
Mrs. Grady
The Dock

Sunday, July 24
US!!!

Maddie got to her feet. "Now let's go interview the neighbors."

Since Mrs. Grady lived next door, they tried her first. But she wasn't home. They decided to try again later. When the Greenbergs also didn't answer, they went to Mr. Barone's house. He was outside, working in his vegetable garden.

He waved to them with his clippers. "Take some tomatoes home!" he called to them. "I have plenty."

"Thanks!" said Maddie.

Atticus took out his casebook.

"We have some questions, Mr. Barone, about the trash that was dumped on your lawn."

"Oh, that." Mr. Barone shrugged. "That's yesterday's news."

"But who do you think did it?" Maddie asked. "Trash was all over our lawn this morning."

"So they hit again." Mr. Barone tugged on a weed. "Don't worry, kids. It's probably some teenagers pulling pranks. They'll get caught before long. In my day we used to TP houses."

" 'TP?' " Atticus said.

"Toilet paper," said Mr. Barone. "We'd throw roll after roll over a house until it was covered in white paper." He shook his head. "It was long, long ago."

He handed a basket of tomatoes
to Maddie. "Enjoy!" he said. "And
share them with your cousin. He told
me this morning that plum tomatoes
are his favorite."

"This morning?" Maddie repeated.

"Yes, he passed by about three hours
ago. Nice kid."

"That's strange," Atticus said after
they thanked Mr. Barone. "Zach doesn't
get up before nine. What was he doing
walking around so early?"

Maddie looked seriously at her
brother. "Get out your list," she said.

Atticus dug out his casebook and
flipped it open.

"When did all this start happening?"
she asked.

"On Thursday," Atticus replied.

Maddie spoke slowly. "And when did Zach first come here?"

Atticus blinked twice and swallowed. "Wednesday night."

"Exactly," said Maddie.

⬥ ⬥ ⬥

On the Case

"**O**ver here," Maddie whispered to her brother. Crouched behind a large sand dune, she looked through her dad's binoculars. "We can keep an eye on Zach, and he won't see us."

After lunch, Zach had mentioned he was going for a walk. Maddie and Atticus decided to follow him. They wanted to see what their teenage cousin was up to. Maybe they would even catch him dumping trash.

"What's he doing?" Atticus asked. They had followed him for half an hour. After walking to the marina, Zach had wandered down to the beach and strolled along the shore. Then he had ended up at a popular picnic spot that was near a cove only locals knew about.

"He's reading," Maddie said. "Why would he come all the way here just to read?"

"Maybe he's meeting someone," Atticus suggested.

"Yes!" Maddie exclaimed. "What if he has a friend who's helping him?"

"Whoa," Atticus said. "Who does he know who would help him? He's only been here for a few days."

"That's what we have to find out,"

Maddie said. Then she gasped.

"What?" Atticus made a grab for the binoculars. Maddie pushed him away.

"It's not Zach," she said. "It's a pod of dolphins splashing in the cove."

"I want to see!" Atticus demanded.

"Let's go down there for a closer look," Maddie suggested. "No one else is there. We'll have them all to ourselves."

They snuck out from behind the dune and made their way down to the sandy cove. At the water's edge, they stopped and stared. It was amazing. The pod was a small one of five dolphins, including one calf.

"How adorable!" Maddie cried, kneeling at the shore.

Atticus crouched beside her.

SAFE HARBOR

A cove is a sheltered area of water. Usually, it has a narrow entrance and land or rocks almost all the way around. Many kinds of plants and animals live in the shallow water of coves.

LEOPARD SHARKS

are named for the spots on their backs. They are gentle and do not bite people.

SEAHORSE mothers lay eggs, but seahorse fathers carry them in pouches on their bellies. When the babies hatch, the father pushes them out of the pouch.

SEA ANEMONES look like flowers, but they're really animals. They wait for fish to swim by, then grab them with their many tentacles (arms).

SEA URCHINS' mouths are underneath their bodies.

The wide, flat bodies of **STINGRAYS** help them glide through the ocean like birds.

OCTOPUSES can change the color of their skin to match their surroundings. This helps them hide.

FLOUNDER lie flat on the bottom of the ocean, waiting for food to swim by. Both their eyes are on the same side of their head.

He pointed to the biggest dolphin. "Is that the dolphin who helped save Zach?" he asked. "That one had a star-shaped scar on its snout, and so does this one."

"I think you're right!" Maddie exclaimed. "And it must be a male dolphin because it's the biggest one in the pod. Look! It's coming over to us."

The big dolphin swam over and chirped at the children.

"He's saying hello," Maddie whispered. "Hi, Star!" She nudged her brother. "Say hello, Atticus."

"I'm not talking to a dolphin. That's silly."

"No, it's not," his sister said. "Dolphins communicate with people all the time."

"If you say so. Nice to see you again, Star."

The dolphin let out a long, cheerful chirp.

"You're right," Atticus said excitedly. "He spoke to me."

The other dolphins swam nearer, although not as close as Star. One of the smaller dolphins touched Star's side and then darted off. The big dolphin gave chase. Soon all the dolphins were enjoying a game of tag.

"This is incredible," Maddie said. "I wish we could join them."

Just then a long, dark shadow loomed over them. Maddie and Atticus whipped around and scrambled to their feet.

• DIS-COVE-RY •

When the tide goes out, many kinds of ocean animals dig into the sand or swim to pools of water left between the rocks. These areas make a cove a good home for saltwater animals that don't swim out to sea.

Sea cucumbers are soft and squishy. Shaped like cucumbers, they come in many different colors.

Sea stars don't have faces, but they do have eyes—one at the tip of each arm.

Purple sea urchins have long, sharp spines and tube-like feet that they use to see!

Horseshoe crabs have existed on Earth since before dinosaurs!

Barnacles produce sticky glue they use to attach themselves to rocks.

When ocean waves crash over a tide pool, mussels close their shells tightly.

There stood Zach, a look of total surprise on his face. "What are you two doing all the way out here? Is anything wrong?"

Atticus gulped. "Nothing's wrong."

"We heard this is a good spot to see dolphins." Maddie pointed at the pod, now playing at the far end of the cove. "And it is. See?"

Zach nodded. "Cool. I just signed up for swimming classes at the community center. Uncle Thomas thinks it's a good idea."

Atticus nodded. "You can't always depend on a dolphin being around to save you."

Maddie and Atticus said goodbye to their cousin and hurried away.

"So he wasn't planning on dumping

trash," Maddie said. "He was here for a swimming class."

Atticus stopped suddenly. "That's what he *says*. Let's see if it's true." He ran up the trail to the park's community center.

When Maddie caught up to him, he was reading a flyer for swim classes on the bulletin board. "Classes don't start until tomorrow," he said.

"Yes, but Zach didn't say he was *taking* a class today," Maddie pointed out. "Just that he signed up for them. And here's his name on the sign-up sheet. He probably came and signed the sheet while we were watching the dolphins."

"It still looks fishy to me," Atticus said. "I'm writing this all down." He took out his casebook.

It was late afternoon by the time
Maddie and Atticus reached town. As
they walked past the main square, they
saw their father standing with a group of
neighbors. The men and women had
angry expressions; a few were shouting.

Before Atticus could ask what was going on, Maddie ran over to the group.

"It's an outrage!" Mrs. Greenberg cried. "Something has to be done to stop this!"

"And right away," Mr. Bazzi said. "The stink will keep my customers away." He pointed to a large heap of rotting garbage in front of his flower shop.

"What happened?" Maddie whispered to her father.

"The Trasher has struck again," he replied. "I was out looking for you guys when I heard a loud noise. It sounded like the crash of metal. Sure enough, when I got here I found the trash bin on its side. Trash was on the ground."

"But who did it? Did you see anyone?" Mrs. Greenberg asked.

"No one," Mr. Cardozo said. "The street was empty. Whoever did this must be a fast runner."

The group worked together to clean up the trash. Then they helped Mr. Bazzi wash down the sidewalk to get rid of the smell. Mr. Bazzi gave Maddie a rose to thank her for her help.

The Cardozos headed down Main Street for home. As their father walked ahead, Atticus whispered to his sister, "You know what this means?"

"What?" Maddie sniffed the flower.

"Zach can't be the Trasher. He was at the park when this trash was dumped."

"That's right," Maddie said.

"There's no way he could have done it."

"But you know who *is* a suspect now?" Atticus didn't wait for an answer. "Dad."

⊾ ⊾ ⊾

Dolphins in Trouble

Early the next morning, Maddie and Atticus went back to the cove. They wanted to see if the dolphins had returned. Morning was a good time to go because the beach wasn't crowded. Their father was already out on his boat. So they'd left a note for Zach— who was still asleep—letting him know where they had gone.

As they walked along the shore, nearing the cove, Maddie remarked,

THE TIDES

Tides come in and go out twice a day. This means the water level at the beach gets higher and lower. At high tide, most of the beach may be underwater. At low tide, the beach is bigger. Seaweed, shells, and other treasures from the ocean may be left behind when the tide goes out.

"I can't believe you actually added our own father as a suspect."

"I had to," Atticus insisted. "A good detective can't rule out *anyone*."

"But what motive would Dad have?"

"I can't think of one," Atticus admitted, "but he's been everywhere the Trasher has struck."

"He's our *only* suspect now that we've cleared Zach."

"True," said Atticus. "Maybe we'll find another suspect today."

Maddie scanned the ocean for a glimpse of the dolphins. "I hope we see the dolphin pod again," she said.

Just then a high-pitched whistle made Atticus cover his ears. "What was that?"

Maddie ran closer to the water. "It's a dolphin!" she cried. "See? It's swimming toward the cove." She peered through the binoculars. "I wonder if that's *our* dolphin. It is! It's Star. And I think he sees us."

"Well, he's in a hurry," Atticus said. "He's swimming really fast."

Both children began to run along the shore. Star swam ahead of them, but every so often he would stop and look back. Was he checking that Maddie and Atticus were following?

By the time they reached the cove, Maddie and Atticus were panting and out of breath.

"I can't run another step," Maddie said.

"You don't have to," Atticus told her. "There's the pod. Why are they swimming in circles?"

"That is strange," Maddie said.

Star joined his pod. He made a series of high-pitched clicks and whistles. The other dolphins answered him, clicking and whistling as they swam in circles.

"Is something wrong with them?" Atticus asked. He spotted a few clouds in the sky. "I heard that animals sometimes know when a storm is coming. Do you think that's it?"

"I don't think so," his sister said. "They would just swim out to sea. It looks like they're in trouble. We have to help them."

STORMY WEATHER

Coastal towns sometimes have big storms called hurricanes in the summer or fall. These storms cause big waves that make the ocean waters dangerous. Strong winds and flooding called storm surge can destroy buildings and docks, damage or sink boats, and wash away lobster traps. Tracking hurricanes is important for fishing boats and the people who work on them.

Marine Fact

HURRICANE KATRINA

The biggest storms are given names so that everyone knows which one is being talked about. Katrina, in 2005, caused terrible flooding.

The speed of the winds as they rotate determines a storm's danger. When it hit land, Katrina was a Category 3 hurricane, which means the wind speeds were 111 to 129 miles per hour.

"We can't help a pod of dolphins," Atticus said. "We should go and get an adult."

Maddie nodded. "I guess you're right. Let's go back to the marina and tell Dad. He should be back by now. He'll know what to do."

But as Maddie and Atticus turned to head back, the dolphins' clicks and whistles got faster and louder.

⛵ ⛵ ⛵

All Tangled Up

Maddie stopped walking. "They don't want us to leave," she said. "What if they're in serious trouble? If we go back to get Dad, it may be too late."

"Then we have to find out why they're so upset," Atticus said. He headed off for the water.

"Wait!" Maddie said. "If you're going in, then so am I."

Together they waded into the cold water. They slowly moved closer to the

dolphins. As the children approached, the dolphins slowed their frantic swimming. Several made low clicks.

Maddie and Atticus didn't get too close to the dolphins. They stopped when the water was waist-high. Maddie peered into the binoculars.

"See anything?" Atticus asked.

"Yes." Maddie moved forward a few steps. "The dolphins are circling around the baby. It's on its side in the water."

"Let me see." Atticus took the binoculars from Maddie. "I think I see the problem." He waited until there was a break in the waves, then splashed back to the shore.

"What is it?" Maddie asked, hurrying after him.

• CIRCLE OF LIFE •

Dolphin mothers usually have one baby, called a calf, at a time. Members of the pod will make a circle around the mother to protect her while she gives birth. When the baby is born, it has to breathe right away. Its mother or another dolphin will help it swim to the surface for air.

"The baby dolphin is caught on something," Atticus said. "I can't see what it is."

"Let's get to the other side of the cove," Maddie suggested. "Maybe we can get a better look from the park."

The two children raced around the cove to the park.

"Look!" Atticus pointed to an overturned trash bin next to a picnic bench. A day's worth of trash—

DINNERTIME

Dolphins use clicking noises to find food. The clicks make an echo when they reach an object. This is called echolocation. It tells dolphins when food is nearby.

Marine Fact

BLOWHOLE

The hole on the top of a dolphin's head is called a blowhole. This lets dolphins breathe while their heads or mouths are in the water.

Dolphins are cooperative hunters. This means they work together to hunt for food.

sandwich scraps, soda cans, and fishing lures—spilled out over the ground. The mess went all the way to the shoreline.

"The Trasher!" Maddie cried.

"No time for that now," Atticus said.

"Wait!" Maddie said. "Maybe *this* is the problem." She bent to pick up a thin, clear string tangled in the trash. It ran down to the water's edge. "It's someone's fishing line," she told Atticus.

"So?" Atticus said.

Maddie peered through the binoculars again. "I think the baby dolphin got tangled up in the line," she said. "That's why it can barely move. Somehow we have to find a way to free the baby dolphin." She gulped. "Before it's too late."

⚓ ⚓ ⚓

Giving Thanks

"**W**e'll need to cut the fishing line," Atticus said.

"With what?" Maddie asked.

"There must be *something* we can use." Atticus started to go through the trash that was strewn around their feet.

Maddie helped him. "What about this?" She held up a metal pop-up tab from a discarded soda can.

Atticus shook his head. "Fishing line is tough to cut. We need something sharp."

MARINE MAMMALS

Dolphins are mammals. So are people. Mammals breathe air using their lungs. Mammal mothers feed their babies milk. Other kinds of mammals also live in the ocean.

The **BLUE WHALE** is the largest animal that has ever lived. A blue whale can be as long as a 737 airplane.

ORCAS are a kind of dolphin. They can eat 500 pounds of food a day. Like other dolphins, they hunt in groups.

SEA LIONS can dive deep to hunt for fish. They can stay underwater for ten to twenty minutes.

Dolphin calves nurse for a few seconds at a time. They do this several times a day.

Some **SEALS** live where the water is cold. They live in large groups—with sometimes up to 1,000 seals!

MANATEES are cousins of elephants. They eat seagrass and other plants. They are gentle and playful.

WALRUSES have extra-long front teeth called tusks. They use their tusks to pull their bodies out of the water.

"My shark tooth!" Maddie touched the tooth that hung on the chain around her neck. "The edges are sharp. I bet it would work."

"Let's try it." Atticus stood, and they both waded into the water.

The dolphins quieted as Maddie and Atticus approached. Again the dolphins slowed down.

"They know we've come to help," Maddie whispered. She didn't want to startle them.

Atticus gulped. "Now what?"

"We have to get close to the baby dolphin," Maddie said.

The calf was floating on one side. It was barely moving. As the children got closer, they saw that the fishing line was wrapped around one of its fins.

"I wonder if the dolphin thought the fishing line was a toy," Atticus said.

"Just like a human baby," Maddie said. She took the shark tooth and waded closer, murmuring the whole time, "Don't worry. I won't hurt you."

"How are you going to cut the line?" Atticus asked. "It's wrapped so tightly around the fin. You might cut the dolphin."

"I'm not going near the dolphin," Maddie said. "Look—part of the line is twisted around this old buoy in the water."

"That's why the baby isn't moving much," Atticus said. "The fishing line pulls it back when it tries to swim away."

Maddie slid the shark tooth between the buoy and the fishing line and began to saw back and forth. "It's working, I think."

"Keep going—it's almost cut through," Atticus said.

Maddie tugged on the line, and it snapped in two.

"Look!" Atticus shouted. The baby dolphin chirped and dove into the water. When it bobbed back up, the fishing line was off its fin and drifting on the water. Atticus grabbed one end of the line and rolled it into a ball. "I'll throw this away when we get home. That way it can't hurt any more dolphins."

The calf splashed the water with its

SAY WHAT?

One way dolphins communicate is by whistling. Every dolphin has its own special way of whistling. Dolphins remember the special whistles of other dolphins they have known for a long time.

fins. It was truly free. Then it swam out of the cove and into the open sea. The rest of the pod followed.

"They probably want to get far away from here after that," Maddie said. "Goodbye, dolphins."

"Don't say goodbye just yet," Atticus said, nodding toward the pod.

Star had turned around and was heading back. He gave each kid a playful nudge. Then he swam away to catch up with the others.

"I think he just thanked us," Atticus said.

"I do, too," said his sister.

⏴ ⏴ ⏴

The Trasher Strikes Again!

Maddie and Atticus waved goodbye to the dolphins until they were silver dots on the horizon.

"Well, we did a good thing," Maddie said. "Let's go home and tell Dad and Zach about it."

"Maybe we'll get our names in the paper!" Atticus's face lit up at the idea.

"Wait!" Maddie held up her hand.

"We're forgetting something."

"What?"

"The trash can. We need to pick up all that trash. We can't leave the park a mess."

Atticus grumbled all the way back to the picnic area. Together the two children picked up the trash.

YUCK!

Garbage on the beach smells bad. And when the tide goes out, it carries the trash with it. This harms ocean water and animals.

CRASH!

Both Maddie and Atticus jumped.

"What was *that*?" Atticus asked.

"It sounded like it was coming from behind those pine trees."

They raced to the scene. By a picnic bench, another trash can lay on its side. More trash was spread all over the ground.

"Oh no!" Atticus cried. "Not again."

"Shhh, not so loud," Maddie whispered. "The Trasher must be nearby."

"You're right," Atticus whispered back. "Now we can catch him for sure."

"I don't know. He—or maybe she— might be dangerous." Maddie gulped. "After all, whoever is doing all this keeps breaking the law—on purpose."

BEACH BUDDIES

Dogs like to run and play on the beach. It's up to you to make sure your dog has a good time and stays safe on the sand.

- Use a leash to keep your dog from running off or bothering other people.

- Bring a plastic bowl and plenty of fresh water, and an umbrella for resting in the shade.

- Bring toys! A tennis ball or other fetch toy will help your pooch have fun in the sun.

Just then they heard a rustling in the shrubs behind them.

"The Trasher!" Atticus shouted, grabbing his sister's arm. "Let's get out of here."

"Where?" Maddie said.

"Anywhere is better than here," Atticus said. "Let's hide out there," he said, pointing to a building.

"Good idea—the community center!"

They took off running. Behind them, they heard thuds and heavy panting.

"Faster!" Maddie cried, but Atticus was already on the porch, doubled over and trying to catch his breath. When he straightened up, he started to laugh.

"Don't stop!" Maddie cried.

Atticus pointed behind her. Maddie turned, and then she started to laugh too.

There was Norville, running, and wagging his long, bushy tail at them.

TRASH TALK

Some animals are scavengers and eat whatever food they can find. Here are some animals that are most likely to get into the trash bin.

RACCOONS can open jars, doors, and trash can lids. They like smelly leftovers like fish and chicken.

 **RATS** will eat almost anything from garbage cans or at the dump.

SKUNKS are smelly pests. They are most active at night and will eat whatever they can find.

 **FLIES** and other insects lay eggs in garbage. When the eggs hatch, rotting scraps provide food for the larvae.

Case Solved

Norville bounded over to Maddie and Atticus. Tangled in his long fur were pieces of deli meat and strands of coleslaw.

"You're a mess," said Maddie, picking some carrot bits off his long ears.

"Looks like our mystery is solved," Atticus said. "Norville is the Trasher."

"Yes, it all makes sense now," Maddie agreed. "The trash problem started on Thursday, the morning after Zach and Norville came to our house."

"And that's why we thought Zach was behind it," Atticus added.

"But the whole time, it was his dog!"

"Norville must have gotten out through the broken screen door," Atticus said. "Smart dog."

"Bad dog!" Maddie said. She turned to Norville and shook her finger at him. "Your days of running wild are over," she said. "Dad will fix the screen door. We'll be putting you on a leash from now on so you can't run away."

Norville raised his shaggy eyebrows as if he understood.

"We'd better go back and pick up the trash," Maddie told her brother.

"This better be the last time," Atticus grumbled.

As they reached the trash bin, Norville ran over. He sniffed for more scraps.

"No," Maddie said firmly. "You're going to be hearing that word a lot more."

Atticus pulled a long rope from the trash. "I can make a leash with this rope," he said.

"Good," Maddie said. "It will be easier to get him home that way."

Atticus made a slipknot and looped the rope over the dog's collar. "There," he said. "No more trash bins for you."

Just then a familiar motorboat raced into the cove and stopped at the dock.

"It's Dad!" Atticus yelled.

"And Zach," Maddie said. "Wait until he finds out what his dog has been up to."

Mr. Cardozo waved at his children.

SEA LEGS

A well-trained dog can enjoy a boating adventure. Everyone gets a life jacket for a safe day at sea.

Marine Fact

GOOD DOG!

Dogs do things that are natural to them. When there's food, they eat it—even if it's in the garbage or on the kitchen counter. They are smart and can learn how to behave. People can train a dog at home, use a dog trainer, or take their pet to special classes to learn how to walk on a leash, sit and stay, and even do tricks.

Everyone in the family can help with training. An open hand helps teach a dog to stay.

"There you are!" he shouted over the roar of the boat's engine. "I was getting worried. Zach told me you left for the cove after breakfast. We thought we'd better come look for you."

"And there's my dog!" Zach cried. He reached out of the boat and stroked Norville. "Where were you all morning?"

"Getting into trouble," Atticus replied.

"We have a *lot* to tell you," Maddie said. "We rescued a baby dolphin . . ."

"And we cracked the Trasher case," Atticus finished.

"And all before noon," their father said. "I'm impressed. Get in the boat and tell us all about it."

The children and Norville piled into the boat.

AHOY!

Coastal waters are perfect places for boating. Whether you want to go fast or slow, have fun or get to work, there's a boat for you.

SPEEDBOAT

FISHING BOAT

ROWBOAT

SAILBOAT

"Where should we begin?" Maddie asked.

"How about at the beginning?" Zach said.

"Okay," Atticus agreed. "It all started on Saturday morning when Mrs. Grady banged on our front door. I spilled the milk I was pouring on my cornflakes and then . . ."

"Oh, brother," Maddie said. "This is going to take *forever*!"

⚓ ⚓ ⚓

GONE FISHING

Oceans, lakes, and ponds are amazing places to explore, learn, and have fun.

animal planet™

Puppy Rescue Riddle

Catherine Nichols
Illustrated by Bryan Langdo

Contents

PUPPY LOVE

Dogs don't speak, but they show how they feel. Some dogs love to be petted, and others like to have their ears rubbed. Your dog may want to cuddle up with you, run around and play, or just hang out.

A Change of Plans

Elliot Flynn looked out his bedroom window. It was a gray, windy Saturday. Gold leaves fell from the beech tree in front of his house and drifted across the lawn. Across the street, two girls were playing a game of catch. Elliot knew their names. Amy Chang and Kyung Lee were in his class. They both seemed nice, even if Amy always had to be right. But he only knew them enough to say hi.

They weren't his friends.

Since school had started in September, he hadn't made one friend. And now it was the end of October. What if he never had anyone to play with? Elliot wished his family had never moved to North Carolina. He had liked his old neighborhood in Virginia just fine.

He let the curtain fall back and sighed. Just then, his brother stepped into the room. Sam had his jacket on and was whistling.

"Are you going out?" Elliot asked his older brother.

"It's almost noon," Sam said. "Time to go to my job."

Sam worked part-time at Adopt-Your-BFF Dog Shelter. He was going to be a vet when he finished school. Sam loved all animals, but he especially loved dogs.

"What about me?" Elliot asked. Their parents were at a movie, and Sam was supposed to be watching him.

Sam tossed a jacket at his brother. "You're coming with me."

"Do I have to?" Elliot had planned to spend the afternoon sorting his rock collection. Yesterday he had found a glittery rock with streaks of purple in it.

"Yes," Sam said. "You're only in second grade. You can't stay home by yourself."

Elliot made a face. But he put on his jacket anyway.

• POPULAR PETS •

Some people prefer dogs to cats. Other people share their homes with fish, birds, and reptiles. Luckily, there are all kinds of pets for all kinds of people.

House cats are hunters, just like lions and tigers. The difference is that smaller cats hunt smaller animals—or catnip toys!

Big or tiny, furry or hairless, long ears or short, dogs come in all shapes and sizes. They are the number one pet in the United States.

The common goldfish, if properly cared for, can grow to be over a foot long. It can weigh as much as 4 pounds.

A guinea pig makes a good first pet because it's easy to care for. Its teeth never stop growing, so it needs hard things to chew on.

Turtles may be slow, but they live a long time. A box turtle can live up to forty years.

Soft and fluffy, with long, floppy ears, rabbits make great pets. You can even teach a rabbit to fetch and to use a litter box.

Outside, Sam and Elliot headed for a white van. The van belonged to the shelter.

Sam used it on weekends
to pick up supplies.

As Sam unlocked the van,
a ball bounced across the street.
"Catch it!" Kyung and Amy
called out.

"Hello," Sam said, turning toward the girls.

"Hi," Kyung answered. She waved shyly to Elliot.

"Are you going to the shelter?" Amy asked. Amy loved dogs too. At school all she ever talked about was dogs, dogs, dogs.

Sam nodded. "But first I have to stop and buy puppy kibble. We just got some puppies, and they need special food."

Amy's and Kyung's eyes lit up when Sam said puppies.

"Puppies!" Amy clapped her hands. "Can we go with you to see them? Please? Pretty please?"

"We won't be any trouble," Kyung promised. "Remember when I came to the shelter to adopt Snowball?"

TAKING CARE

A doctor who treats animals is called a veterinarian, or vet for short. Some vets care for pets, such as dogs, cats, and rabbits. Other vets look after farm animals, such as sheep, goats, and horses. And vets who work in zoos keep elephants, tigers, and all the other animals healthy.

Pet Fact

BECOMING A VET

To become a vet, first you have to go to college and take a lot of science classes. Then you have four more years of vet school. This is when you get to work directly with animals. In your last year of vet school, you will take a special test. If you pass, you will get your license to practice veterinary medicine. Congratulations!

Snowball was Kyung's new dog. She was just a few months old.

Sam looked at the two girls and nodded. "Okay," he said. "You can keep Elliot company."

"Yay!" the girls cried.

"But first we have to ask your parents."

While Sam, Amy, and Kyung went to check with the girls' parents, Elliot sat inside the van and stared at the cloudy sky. The gray day matched his mood. All he had wanted to do this Saturday was sort through his rock collection. Instead, he was on his way to a dog shelter. Elliot would never admit it out loud, but dogs scared him a little. He sighed. It was going to be a long afternoon.

Wiggly Balls of Fur

Adopt-Your-BFF was down a steep hill, at the bottom of a valley. As soon as Sam had parked, Kyung and Amy rushed out of the van and ran inside. Elliot helped his brother. Together, they carried bags of puppy food into the small one-story building. Sam stopped at the front desk to say hi to Tina, the shelter's manager. Elliot stayed near his brother. He read a poster that hung behind the desk: *Adopt Your BFF Today!*

Kyung and Amy were already in the back area where the dogs were kept. Rows of cages were stacked on top of each other. The larger bottom cages held two big dogs. Some smaller and medium-size dogs filled the upper cages.

Kyung counted all the animals. "When I adopted Snowball, there were a lot more dogs," she said. "Now there are only seven dogs and six puppies."

Tina overheard her. "That's because we had a big adoption fair last weekend. Most of our dogs found good homes."

Amy peered into the cage with the six puppies. Three were all white, and two were tan with splotches of black.

The tiniest puppy was a pretty copper color. The puppies yipped and stepped over one another.

"They are sooo cute!" Amy cooed.

"How old are they?" Kyung asked.

"They're about ten weeks old," Sam said. He unlocked the cage.

Amy scooped up the tiny copper puppy. "This one is my favorite," she said. "I'm going to call her Penny."

Sam gently lifted a puppy with a splotch of black over its eye from the cage. "But she isn't yours," he reminded Amy. He gave Kyung the puppy to hold.

"Not yet," Amy said. "But my parents have been promising that I can get a dog someday. They just *have to* let me have her."

Elliot shook his head. He couldn't understand what the fuss was about. The puppies were cute, sure. They were wiggly balls of fur with big dark eyes. But they also demanded a lot of attention. And the one Kyung was holding had just nipped her fingers.

"Ouch!" Kyung gave the puppy back to Sam.

"Puppies this age like to bite," Sam told her. "It's natural."

"I know," Kyung said. "Snowball nipped when we first got her. But we trained her to stop."

Sam held out the black-and-tan puppy to Elliot. "Would you like to hold him?"

Elliot put up a hand. "No, thanks,"

IT'S PLAYTIME!

It is important to play with your puppy for at least 20 minutes every day and give them at least 30 minutes of exercise. Playtime is a great way to bond with your puppy, and it's very fun!

he said. He didn't want a puppy gnawing on his fingers.

Sam put both puppies back in the cage with the rest of the litter. Then he opened the cage below. A big dog poked its head out and sniffed the air.

Elliot backed away.

"This is Toby," Sam said. "He's very gentle."

Toby slowly came out of the cage and thumped his bushy tail against Sam's leg.

"It's been years since Toby was a puppy," Sam said. "He was an older dog when his family left him with us."

"Why did they leave him?" Elliot asked.

"The new apartment they were moving to didn't allow pets," Sam explained.

Elliot swallowed hard. That must have been rough. He wondered if Toby missed his family.

"Toby doesn't get much attention, not the way the puppies do," Sam said. "Would you like to spend some time with him, Elliot?"

Elliot didn't answer right away. Toby was a *big* dog. He came all the way up to Sam's thigh. But Sam had said he was gentle. "Okay," he whispered.

Leaving the girls fussing over the puppies, Sam led Toby and Elliot to a quiet area in the back of the building. Toby flopped on the rug, and Elliot sat down next to him. The big dog rested his head on Elliot's knee. Elliot stroked his silky ears, and Toby let out a sigh.

A LOOK INSIDE

Most of the animals in a typical animal shelter are dogs and cats. But some shelters take in birds, rabbits, and other pets. When an animal first enters the shelter, a vet gives it a checkup. The vet will make sure the animal is healthy. If there is a problem, the vet will try to fix it.

Staff and volunteers look after the animals. They give the animals food and water and clean their cages or pens. They walk the dogs and cuddle the cats.

PICK ME!

Before you can adopt a pet, you have to fill out an application and answer questions. Then a volunteer will take you to see the animals. After you have picked out a pet, you will sign a contract. The contract says the adopter promises to take good care of the animal.

Pet Fact

"He likes it!" Elliot said, surprised.

"He sure does," Sam said.

While Elliot was petting Toby, Sam unloaded the rest of the bags of puppy food from the van. Kyung and Amy were following Tina around the shelter. She showed the girls how to scoop the right amount of puppy kibble. She even let them feed the puppies. Elliot preferred to stay with Toby. He scratched behind the dog's silky ears, and Toby wriggled and let out a big yawn. He seemed happy.

🐾 🐾 🐾 🐾

The bell on the front door tinkled, and a man walked in. He had gray hair and sad, droopy eyes. In his arms was a large cardboard box.

"Hi, Mr. Rooney," Sam said. "What's that you have?"

"Just a few things," the man said gruffly. "Some canned dog food, leashes, a few toys." He placed the box on the front desk. "They were Quincy's. I thought your place could put them to good use."

"Thanks," Tina said. "We can always use more supplies. And I'm sorry about Quincy. He was a great dog."

"Yeah, well." Mr. Rooney shrugged.

At the sound of Mr. Rooney's voice, Toby's ears perked up. The old dog lifted himself slowly off the rug. Then he ambled to Mr. Rooney's side.

"Do you want to see the new puppies?" Amy asked. "They're adorable."

"Not interested," he said quickly.

He bent down to pet Toby, then left.

Tina shook her head. "He's still upset about Quincy. He loved that dog."

"What happened?" Kyung asked.

"Mr. Rooney's dog died a few months ago," Sam said. "They did everything together."

"That's so sad," Amy said.

Tina sighed. "It is. But Quincy lived a long, happy life." She slipped on her jacket. "I have to get going," she told Sam. "Will you lock up when you leave?"

"Sure thing," Sam said. "I'm almost done with my chores. Then I have to get these kids home."

While Sam finished feeding the dogs, Elliot took the box off the counter and looked through it. There were throw toys, a tangle of leashes, and cans of dog food. At the very bottom, buried under some rawhide bones, was some kind of book. Elliot dug it out. It smelled musty, but that didn't stop him from opening it. The book was all about rocks and how to identify them. He was thumbing through the pages when Sam called to them.

"Let's get a move on, kids," he said. "It's late, and I promised Amy's and Kyung's parents I'd have them home by now."

Elliot hurried to put on his jacket. Without thinking, he slipped the book in his pocket.

Riddle Me This

O n the ride home, the drizzle of rain turned into a downpour. The van's windshield wipers swished back and forth at top speed. Elliot peered out the window at the two-lane highway. He listened to Amy talk to her mother on Sam's cell phone.

"And the littlest dog was so cute," she said. "She's the one I want. Please, Mom? Pretty please?"

Elliot noticed how tightly Amy's hand gripped the phone.

"But why?" Amy cried. "You promised I could have a dog."

After some more back-and-forth, Amy said goodbye to her mother. "She said puppies are a lot of work."

"They sure are," Sam said over his shoulder.

"My mom said first I have to prove that I'm responsible enough."

Kyung patted her friend's arm. "You can help me take care of Snowball. That will show your parents that you're ready for a dog."

But Amy just shook her head and stuck out her bottom lip. "I'll never get a dog. Never." Her eyes brimmed with tears.

Elliot reached for a tissue. He twisted in his seat to hand it to Amy.

A BUSY DAY

Good morning! What are the puppies doing today at the rescue center?

Arf! Arf! It's time for breakfast.

Scrub-a-dub! This puppy needs a bath.

Picture day! A photo of this sweet puppy will go on the adoption website.

Let's play! The puppies run around the fenced-in yard.

Cuddle up! These puppies found their forever family.

The hard edge of the book in his jacket poked his side. He pulled it out. Maybe there was something in the book to cheer up Amy. He flipped through the musty pages, and an old yellowed envelope fell out.

Elliot opened the envelope. Inside was a single sheet of loose-leaf paper with words handwritten in faded purple ink. Elliot read the first two sentences: " 'Answer the riddle below. It will lead you to a great treasure.' " Underneath was a riddle.

> What do you put in a bucket to make it lighter?

"What did you say?" Kyung asked. Elliot realized he had read the riddle out loud. He repeated it. Then he showed Kyung and Amy the book and the sheet of paper.

"That's strange," Amy said, drying her eyes on her sleeve.

"What do you think the treasure is?" Kyung asked. "A precious jewel?"

"Maybe it's a chest filled with gold," Amy said.

"Or maybe it's a piece of gum," Sam said from the front seat. "It sounds like someone is pulling your leg." He stopped at a light. "Wow," he added, "this rain is really coming down."

Elliot repeated the riddle a third time. " 'What do you put in a bucket to make it lighter?' " He scratched his chin. "Any ideas?"

A VISIT TO THE VET

The vet will ask you questions about your pet's health and behavior. Is your pet eating? Is it active? Are there any problems? Next, the vet will check your pet's fur—a shiny coat means a healthy animal. Then the vet will look at your pet's eyes and ears. The eyes should be clear, and the ears, clean. A vet will also look inside your pet's mouth to make sure the teeth are in good shape. Next, the vet may listen to your pet's heart and lungs with a stethoscope. The vet will also weigh your pet and take its temperature. If it needs any shots or medicine, the vet will give them. Now the visit to the vet is over. You can take your pet home—until checkup time again next year.

"That's easy," Amy answered. "Air."

"I don't think that's it," Kyung said. "How would you put air in a bucket?"

"Besides," Elliot said, "air has weight."

"It does not," Amy said.

Elliot was about to argue when Sam pulled over and stopped the van.

"What happened?" Kyung asked.

A state trooper was walking over to them. Sam opened his window just enough to talk to the trooper without letting too much rain into the van.

"What's the problem, officer?" he asked politely. "This is some really nasty weather, isn't it?"

The trooper nodded. Rain dripped off his hat. "Yep," he said. "This storm came up all of a sudden. We weren't expecting so much rain. It caused the creek to overflow. Now the road up ahead is flooded. We just closed it. You'll have to turn around and go back the way you came."

"I'm trying to get to Greenville," Sam told him.

"Take the exit over by Pine Valley," the trooper advised. "That road is safe."

Sam thanked the officer and closed his window. Then he slowly made a U-turn and drove back in the direction they'd come.

Elliot looked out the foggy window. In front of an abandoned shed, he could see a rusty watering can. Water poured out from its spout. "A hole!" he shouted.

Amy and Kyung turned to stare at him.

"The answer to the riddle," he explained. " 'What do you put in a bucket to make it lighter?' "

"A hole!" Amy and Kyung sang out.

Elliot stared at the riddle in his hand. "But how does the answer lead to treasure?" he wondered aloud.

Dangerous Weather

After driving several miles, they were about to pass by the animal shelter. The rain was still coming down hard, and Sam was driving slowly.

"I hope the puppies are safe," Amy shouted over the sound of the rain hitting the roof and the slapping windshield wipers.

The building had been built on low ground. While the road was still safe to drive on, the water was quickly filling the valley below.

Elliot thought of Toby sleeping in the big cage below the puppies. What if the water seeped under the door and started to rise? Toby would be trapped. "We have to stop!" he cried.

His brother was already turning into the drive that led to the shelter. "The dogs are okay for now," Sam told them. "But I don't like how fast the water is rising. If the creek overruns its banks, the building will flood for sure."

"What can we do?" Kyung asked.

Sam pulled out his cell phone. "I'm calling Tina." He dialed. "Hi, Tina," he said when she answered. He explained about the rising water. "We have to get the animals out of the shelter," he told her. "It's not safe for them—or us—to stay here." He listened and nodded his head. "That's a good idea," he said. He put away his phone.

"What's a good idea?" Amy demanded.

"Tina reminded me that Frank Rooney has a cabin on high ground not far from here. It's right up the road. We can take the dogs there until the storm quiets down. Are you ready to help?"

"Yes!" all three kids shouted.

Covering their heads with their jackets, they dashed into the building and got to work. Kyung packed up the food for the dogs and puppies. Amy put the puppies into a crate, and the kids brought it to the van. Elliot helped

Sam leash the older dogs and walk
them into the van. Once inside, they
strapped all seven dogs into safety
harnesses.

Toby was the last one in.

The rain didn't seem to bother him, but he walked slowly.

"His legs are stiff," Sam explained. "He's an old dog. When it rains like this, his joints hurt."

Elliot stroked Toby's fur and gave him a thick blanket to rest on. Then all three kids climbed into the van.

"My sneakers are soaked," Amy said.

"So are mine," Kyung said. "And my hair is wet too. I hope Mr. Rooney has a lot of towels."

"What if he isn't home?" Elliot asked.

"Don't worry," Sam said. "Tina told me he leaves a key under the mat for emergencies." He drove slowly up the steep mountain road. "And this certainly is an emergency."

FROM HERE TO THERE

It's not always easy to move an animal from one place to another. Many animals get nervous when they travel. That's why it is important to make the trip comfortable and safe for everyone.

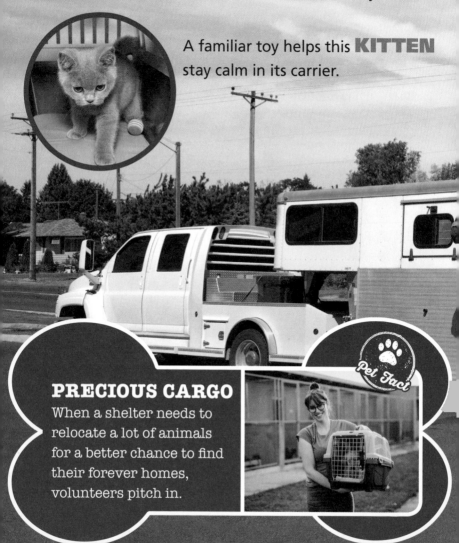

A familiar toy helps this **KITTEN** stay calm in its carrier.

PRECIOUS CARGO
When a shelter needs to relocate a lot of animals for a better chance to find their forever homes, volunteers pitch in.

Pet Fact

This **DOG** is traveling by plane to its new home. The large, sturdy carrier helps it stay safe during the flight.

This clever **CAT** found a special way to travel. How do you think the horse feels?

HORSES ride in special trailers where they have plenty of room to move and hay to eat.

Before starting the van, Sam passed his phone to Amy. "You and Kyung need to call your parents and tell them there's been a change in plans. I don't want them to worry. Tell them that I'll drive you home after we get the dogs settled."

By the time the girls had finished speaking to their parents, the group had made the short trip up the hill to the small cabin.

Mr. Rooney was on the front porch. He had on a long raincoat, a hat, and rubber boots. He looked surprised when Sam stepped out of the van.

"What are you doing up here?" he asked.

Sam quickly filled him in on the

situation. "And so," he ended, "we hoped you would let the dogs stay in the cabin until the storm breaks."

Mr. Rooney frowned and looked at all the dogs in the back of the van. Some were barking to be let out.

"I was just going up the road," he said. "I need to check on my neighbor. Sometimes her generator goes out in storms."

"That's kind of you," Sam said.

"Well, we've been neighbors a long time," Mr. Rooney replied. "This cabin has been in my family for ages. I used to come up here when I was just a boy."

"So . . . about the dogs?" Sam asked. "They won't cause any trouble. I promise."

• WALKING THE DOG •

All dogs need exercise. Going on walks is a fun way to spend time with your best friend. For safety, be sure to always put a leash on your dog. And it's a good idea to bring water and a bowl with you in case your dog gets thirsty.

Pet Fact

WHAT TO WEAR?

In colder weather, dogs without thick fur might need a sweater or coat. Dogs don't need to wear anything in the summer. But you should walk your dog in the mornings or evenings when it's cooler.

Mr. Rooney stared into the back of the van. Toby's head was pressed against the back window. His tongue was out, and he was panting. "Yes, the dogs can stay. I won't be away for long."

"Thank you," Sam said.

"And I want you and the kids to stay here, too," Mr. Rooney added. "No sense in you driving in a storm like this. Here's my number if you need anything. Wait here until it passes. Then you can be on your way."

Sam nodded. "We'll do that," he said. "Sorry to cause you trouble."

"No trouble," Mr. Rooney said gruffly.

A Missing Puppy

The children helped Sam bring the dogs into the cabin. They dried off the wet animals, then themselves. Toby settled into a warm spot in front of the screened fireplace.

Sam laughed. "You stay right here, Toby, and warm your old bones." He patted the big dog's head. "Amy, you can let the puppies out of the crate. They need some exercise. I'm taking the rest of the dogs into the bedroom."

Even though the log cabin was small,

there was plenty for the puppies to do. As soon as Amy opened the crate, they dashed out. They scampered across the wood floor and began chasing each other. Amy and Kyung clapped in delight.

Elliot plopped beside Toby. The old dog kept his eyes on the frisky puppies. When one skidded into him, Toby gave the puppy a lick and nudged her away.

Kyung had a ball in her pocket. She tossed it gently, and the puppies ran after it. They chased the rolling ball all through the cabin—down the hallway, into the open kitchenette, and into the mudroom. Their excited yapping filled the cabin.

Sam came out of the bedroom. He scooped up two puppies, one in each hand. "You guys need to go back in your crate,"

he said. "You're getting too excited." He

gently placed the furry balls into the crate.

"Help me get the rest
of the puppies," Sam
said to Kyung and Amy.

Elliot stroked Toby's ears and

watched Kyung and Amy chase the

puppies around the room.

"Here are two more," Kyung said.

"And I have another," Amy said. She scrunched her nose. "But shouldn't there be one more? Where's Penny, the tiny copper puppy?"

Sam counted the puppies in the crate. Five. One puppy was missing. "She must be hiding," he said. "All hands on deck. You, too, Elliot. We have to find her."

Sam and the kids searched the cabin. No puppy.

"Where can she be?" Amy wailed.

Kyung bit her lip. She looked like she wanted to say something.

Sam looked puzzled. "Amy," he said, "at the shelter, you put the puppies in the crate. Are you sure you got all of them?"

NEIGH!
"Here I am!
Pay attention
to me!"

Animals can't speak, of course. But that doesn't mean they don't communicate. Your pet may be telling you something important. You just have to know how to listen.

**SQUEAK!
SQUEAK!**
"Feed me!"

Your cat purrs when it is relaxed and happy. Squeaks mean your guinea pig wants food, and chirps and whistles mean it's happy to see you. A dog may bark as a warning. It will also bark to let you know it needs something—a walk or a favorite toy. Or maybe it's time for dinner.

HISS!
"Go away!"

"I think so," Amy said. "But we were in a hurry. There was so much going on. I can't remember if I counted them."

"I don't think you did," Kyung whispered.

Amy looked stricken. "What if the puppy is still at the shelter?"

Another Riddle

Sam hurried over to the coatrack. He put on one of Mr. Rooney's spare rain jackets. "It wasn't your fault," he told Amy. "We were all in a hurry. I should have checked the crate too." He zipped up his jacket. "I'll drive back to the shelter and see if the puppy is there."

Amy gasped. "What do you mean *if*?" she asked. "The puppy has to be at the shelter. Where else could she be?"

"I don't remember seeing her in the

cage," Kyung said. "Do you?"

Amy shook her head, and her lower lip trembled. "I don't remember!"

"Don't worry," Sam said, patting her on the shoulder. "We'll find her. The shelter is just down the road. I won't be long."

"Can't we go with you?" Amy begged. "We can help you find her."

"No," said Sam. "Mr. Rooney will be back soon. But until he's here, I need you to stay and look after the dogs. The telephone is over there." He pointed to an old-fashioned phone on the desk in the hallway. "Call me if there's a problem. You know my number, Elliot."

After Sam left, the three kids stared at each other. They were all thinking the same thing: where was the missing puppy—and was she okay?

Outside, the wind howled. A flash of lightning lit up the gloom. It was followed quickly by a loud crack.

The three kids jumped.

"It was probably just a falling tree branch," Elliot said bravely. He hoped he sounded calmer than he felt. His heart was racing. Kyung and Amy were clinging to each other.

"Let's search one more time," Elliot suggested. He figured that being busy would keep their minds off the storm. "Remember how the puppies were running around? Maybe the puppy got stuck somewhere."

"Good idea," said Kyung. "Let's look for her together, Amy."

But Amy shook her head. "It's my fault," she said in a low voice. "My mom is right. I'm not responsible enough to have a dog."

Kyung hugged her friend. "That's not what she said. She said you have to *show* her you're responsible. So start looking."

Amy nodded, and the three kids examined every inch of the cabin. They looked behind the refrigerator and stove. They crawled under tables and opened cupboards. But they didn't find the puppy.

Elliot sank on the rug next to Toby. The big dog licked his hand. "I guess she's not here," Elliot said at last.

Kyung nodded.

• WEATHER OR NOT? •

With their extra-sharp senses, some animals may be able to anticipate weather changes before we do. A dog can hear rumblings of thunder long before the sound reaches our ears, and it may bark or hide. How do other animals behave when bad weather is coming?

SHEEP run when frightened. But they often huddle together during bad weather.

BIRDS sense air pressure changes that signal a storm is on the way, and they fly low to avoid strong winds.

FROGS croak more loudly and longer when bad weather is coming to attract potential mates.

COWS lie down to stay warm. This often happens when the temperature drops before a rainstorm.

"Then why hasn't Sam called to say he's found her?" Amy's dark eyes were wide with worry.

Elliot wished he could get everyone's mind off the puppy. Then he remembered the paper with the riddle. He pulled it from his jeans pocket and unfolded it. "I still don't get how the riddle leads to treasure," he said.

Kyung looked around the cabin. "The book was in the box of supplies Mr. Rooney brought to the shelter, right?"

Elliot nodded.

"Then maybe the treasure is somewhere in the cabin. Didn't he say the cabin has been in his family for years and years?"

Amy stood up. "The answer to the riddle was a hole in a bucket." She walked over to a framed print hanging on the wall. It showed a girl with a bucket milking a cow. Amy peered at the picture. "There's a tiny hole in the bucket," she said excitedly. "It looks like it was made with a pin."

Kyung and Elliot got up to look.

Amy took the print off the wall and turned it over. A piece of notebook paper was folded and taped to the other side.

"What are you waiting for?" Kyung cried. "Open it and see what it says."

Bad News

Amy carefully removed the yellowed strip of tape. Then she unfolded the paper. "This note is written in purple ink, too," she said.

"Read it!" Elliot said.

" 'Good for you,' " Amy read. " 'You found the answer to the riddle. Now here is another one.' "

> What has eighty-eight keys but can't open any doors?

Elliot shook his head. "It beats me.

What good are keys if you can't open a door?"

"Keys aren't just for opening doors," Amy reminded him. "There are keys that open safes or diaries."

"Good thinking," Elliot said.

Kyung giggled.

"What's so funny?" Amy asked her friend.

"I can't believe you don't know the answer," Kyung said.

"You do?" Elliot said.

"Of course," Kyung said.

"Well, are you going to tell us what it is?" Amy tapped her foot impatiently.

"It's a piano!" Kyung sang out proudly. "I should know. I take lessons on one every week."

STORM PREP

Big storms can seem scary for people and pets. The best way to get through them is to stay calm and be prepared. Here are some tips to keep you and your family safe the next time a storm hits.

- If your pet is afraid of storms, talk to your vet about ways to help it cope.

- During a storm, stay indoors and away from windows.

- Listen for weather alerts and updates on your radio or TV.

- Have batteries and flashlights on hand in case the power goes out.

- Keep a first aid kit in the house and car. Some items to include are bandages, scissors, medicine, hand sanitizer, safety pins, and a blanket.

- Keep a packed overnight bag handy in case you need to leave quickly. Think about what you'll need, such as pajamas, a book, and clothes. And don't forget a bag for pets that includes food and water, bowls, and a leash or travel crate.

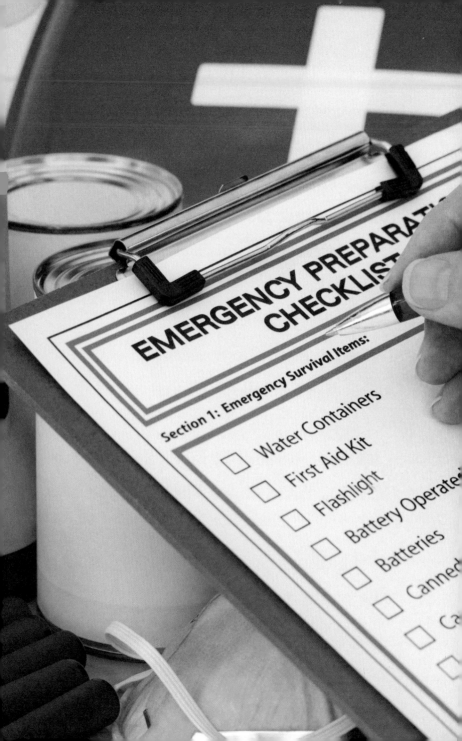

Elliot groaned. It seemed so obvious now.

But Amy wasn't satisfied. "What kind of clue is that?" she demanded. "Look around. Do you see a piano?"

It was true. A piano couldn't fit in the small cabin.

Just then the telephone rang. Elliot stepped over to the desk and picked up the receiver. "Hello?" He listened for a long time.

"Okay," he said at last. "Don't worry about us. We're okay." He hung up the phone.

"That was Sam," he told the girls. "The puppy wasn't at the shelter."

Amy shook her head. "That can't be," she said. "Where else could she be?

•WHERE CAN IT BE?•

Everybody loses things. Maybe you lost your glasses or your favorite pen. Or maybe you can't find the homework that's due on Monday. The first thing to do is to stay calm. Take a deep breath and clear your mind.

STEP 1

Try to remember when you last had the object.

STEP 2

Retrace your steps.

STEP 3

If you still can't find what you're looking for, ask other people. Maybe they know where it is.

STEP 4

Still no luck? Then take a break. Sometimes when you stop looking for a lost object, that's when you find it.

She's not here. We looked and looked."

Another bolt of lightning filled the room. It was followed by thunder.

"What if she's outside in the storm?" Amy cried.

Kyung put her arms around her friend. "When will Sam be back?" she asked.

"That's the other problem," Elliot said. "His van stalled in all this rain. He's trying to fix it, but he said it might be awhile."

Kyung gulped. "I'm getting scared," she confessed. "I just want to go home."

"But what about Penny?" Amy said. "We have to find her."

"Sam called Mr. Rooney and told him about the missing puppy and the van. Mr. Rooney is on his way. He should be here in about ten minutes," Elliot said. "Maybe he'll have some ideas."

CRASH!

Outside, a tree branch fell.

Amy clutched Kyung's arm. "I hope he gets here soon," she said.

Elliot didn't answer. He was staring at something on the desk. Next to the phone was a gold music box in the shape of a piano. He picked it up and showed it to the girls. "Here's the piano."

The Final Riddle

Elliot turned the music box upside down. But there wasn't a piece of paper taped to the bottom.

"Open the lid," Kyung said.

Elliot did. "I don't see anything," he said. He showed them the smooth red velvet under the lid.

"I don't care about this silly game!" Amy cried. "I just want to find Penny." She went and gazed into the crate.

The five puppies were sleeping in a pile. Amy looked at them and sighed.

Kyung took the music box from Elliot. "I have one of these," she said. She gently lifted the velvet compartment. Underneath, next to the mechanism that played the musical notes, was a small folded piece of paper. Carefully, Kyung took it out and handed it to Elliot.

Taking a deep breath, Elliot read the riddle.

> This is the last riddle. If you succeed, you will find the treasure. What has hands but cannot clap?

Amy looked up from the puppies. "Read that again," she demanded.

WRITE A RIDDLE

A riddle is a puzzling question that needs to be solved. Would you like to make your own riddle? Here's how:

First, decide what the answer to your riddle will be. It can be an animal or an object or a place—anything.

Then make a list of words that describe your answer.

Write a sentence for each word.

Now give your riddle to a friend. Can your friend solve the riddle?

For example, if you picked a squirrel as your answer, your riddle might look like this:

It's an animal.
It has a bushy tail.
It likes to eat acorns.
It lives in the forest.
What is it?

Elliot repeated, " 'What has hands but cannot clap?' "

"I know," Amy said. Her eyes lit up. "It's a clock, right? It has to be a clock."

"Yes!" Kyung said. "That makes sense."

"So where's a clock?" Elliot asked.

The three kids looked around the cabin. A wall clock hung in the kitchenette. But when they took it down, nothing was taped to it.

"Maybe it's *inside* the clock," Amy said.

Elliot shook his head. "I don't want to break Mr. Rooney's clock."

"I think I remember seeing another clock," Kyung said. "It was when we were looking for the puppy." She walked over to the mudroom at the back of the cabin.

Amy and Elliot followed her.

A tall grandfather clock stood against one wall. The base of the clock had a small door. Kyung crouched and opened it.

Elliot and Amy held their breath.

Kyung shook her head. "It's empty," she reported. "Maybe someone already found the treasure a long time ago."

Elliot nodded. He felt disappointed. They had solved all the riddles but hadn't found the treasure. He walked over to the back window and looked out onto the garden. "The storm finally stopped," he said. "It's just drizzling now."

"Yay!" Kyung shouted.

Amy held up her hand. "Be quiet!" she ordered. "I heard something."

The three kids listened. Faint but steady yapping came from the clock.

"That's strange," Kyung said. "A clock that barks?"

"That's not the clock!" Amy cried. "That's the puppy!" She dropped to her knees and stuck her head in the open compartment. "Penny, where are you?"

A louder yap answered her.

"Maybe she's *behind* the clock," Elliot said. "Help me move it."

Carefully, the three children inched the giant clock farther away from the wall. No puppy.

"But I can hear her!" Amy wailed.

Elliot shook his head. "The yapping isn't coming from the clock," he said. "Listen."

Puppies are curious and like to explore. This is especially true when they find themselves in new places. They may jump up on furniture and counters, chew your favorite shoes, steal food, and bite and tug on things and people. They need plenty of exercise and training to outgrow these puppy behaviors. And just like young children, they need to be watched so they don't get into trouble.

Puppies and kids love to be messy together!

The children stood still, not talking.

Yap! Yap! Yap!

"It's coming from inside the wall!" Kyung shouted.

Elliot examined the paneled wall around the clock carefully. Every few feet he knocked on the wood.

"What are you doing?" Amy asked.

"Shh," Elliot said. "I need to find where the wall isn't solid." A few feet from the clock, he knocked again. Instead of a dull thud, the sound was hollow.

"This is it!" he cried. He pointed to a narrow door that came up to his waist. The door blended in so well with the wood that it was almost impossible to see.

"It's a trapdoor," he explained. "I bet it goes to the attic. We have one at our house."

"But how did Penny get in there?" Amy asked.

Elliot shrugged. "She must have managed to open the door with her paw."

"I see scratches in the wood," Kyung said. She pointed to faint marks at the bottom of the door.

Elliot nodded. "And it's pretty drafty in here. The wind might have slammed the door shut and trapped her inside."

"Just get her out!" Amy wailed.

There wasn't a doorknob. So Elliot felt around the wood panels until he found an opening. He wedged his fingers

inside and pulled. The door popped open.
Out sprang a yapping furry ball.

Amy scooped the tiny, trembling
puppy into her arms. "Penny!" she cried.

Treasure at Last

Penny was licking Amy's face when the back door opened. Mr. Rooney stepped into the mudroom. He looked at the grandfather clock and the opened trapdoor and frowned. But he didn't say a word.

Elliot scrambled to his feet. "We can explain, Mr. Rooney," he said.

"I'm sure you can," Mr. Rooney said. He took off his raincoat and hat and placed them on hooks. "But first I need a hot cup of cocoa. What about you?"

Ten minutes later, the children were sipping hot cocoa. They told Mr. Rooney about their adventures.

Mr. Rooney chuckled. "You found the envelope in my old book?"

Elliot showed him the first riddle.

"I can remember writing this," Mr. Rooney told them.

Amy looked up from petting Penny. "*You* wrote the riddles?"

"Yes," Mr. Rooney said. "When I was not much older than you. My cousin Tim was visiting, and I thought it would amuse him."

"So Tim never found the treasure?" Kyung asked.

Mr. Rooney shook his head. "All Tim

wanted to do was fish and play cards."
He shrugged. "So I tucked away the
envelope in the book I was reading and
forgot all about it."

"So where is the treasure?" Kyung
asked. "We didn't find any."

"Yes, we did," Amy said sharply. She
picked up Penny and gave her a kiss.
"We found the most important treasure
of all."

"That, you did," Mr. Rooney said
with a smile. "But there *is* another
treasure."

Elliot jumped to his feet and ran to
the mudroom. The girls followed.

Elliot poked his head inside the
trapdoor. "I don't see anything," he said.

"That's because you're not looking in

the right place," Mr. Rooney told him. "Remember the last riddle."

"But the treasure wasn't in the grandfather clock," Kyung said.

Elliot stared at the tall clock. Then he dragged a chair over to it. He climbed up and stood on tiptoes. He reached up and felt around the top of the clock.

"I got it!" he cried.

Mr. Rooney helped him bring down a battered cardboard box. "Open it," Mr. Rooney said.

Elliot lifted the lid. Inside, it was packed with objects from nature: rocks with glittery specks in them, dried leaves, pine cones, and many other wonders.

TREASURE HUNTING

It can be lots of fun to go treasure hunting in your backyard or neighborhood. Make sure to bring a camera with you to take pictures of anything that catches your eye. You can also bring a notebook to make notes about where you found the treasures, but make sure you leave everything where you found it!

"Everything I collected came from the woods around the cabin," Mr. Rooney said proudly.

Elliott picked up a shiny rock and examined it closely. "I collect rocks, too," he said.

Mr. Rooney picked up the box and handed it to Elliot. "Then you should have this," he said.

"I can't take it!" Elliot said. "It's yours."

"But you played my game and won."

"We all did," Elliot said. "Kyung and Amy solved the riddles too." He turned to the two girls. "We could share it," he said shyly.

"No, thank you," Amy said. "I already have my treasure." She snuggled Penny.

Kyung kneeled beside Elliott.
"I'd like to share," she said. "I collect leaves."

"Great!" Elliot smiled at her.

ADOPTION OPTIONS

When you go to an animal shelter to adopt a pet, it's easy to fall in love with all the animals. It can be hard to make a decision. So before you go, discuss with your family what you're looking for in an animal companion. Then shelter workers can help match you up with the perfect pet for you.

PUPPY

Puppies are high energy! They tend to cause or get into trouble. And they need to be house-trained. Does your family have the time and patience for a puppy?

TEENAGER

Dogs become "teenagers" at around six months. This may last for a few months or a year. These youngsters like to explore the world. They can sometimes be unpredictable and may still need some training.

ADULT

Dogs are considered grown-ups at one or two years old. They retain their curiosity and energy, but are more calm. Most can fit into family life easily.

SENIOR

Older dogs make wonderful companions. They may develop medical issues that need attention, but mostly they want to love and be loved.

DECEMBER

2

National Mutt Day!

Pet Fact

WHAT'S A MUTT?

Mutts are unique mixes of multiple breeds. Many people think mutts are likely to be healthier in the long run. Purebred dogs have traits that are specific to a particular breed.

More Surprises

The rest of the afternoon passed quickly. Sam returned. He had fixed the van, but many roads were still flooded. Mr. Rooney invited them to stay until it was safe to drive.

Sam was surprised and happy to see Penny curled up in Amy's lap. The children told him how they had rescued the puppy from her hiding place.

"You were all very responsible," Sam said. "I'm proud of you."

SUPERSIZE!
No matter how big your puppy gets, it may still try to fit on your lap.

After they fed and walked all the dogs, Mr. Rooney popped some popcorn. Then he sat in his easy chair and told them stories about when he was a boy. Many of his stories were about the fun he'd had exploring the woods and the treasures he had found there.

He told the children about all the animals he had spotted, including a friendly chipmunk that lived in the woodpile. As he talked, Toby came over and rested his snout on his knee. Mr. Rooney petted the old dog. Every now and then, he sneaked him a piece of popcorn.

Sam stepped outside to call Kyung's and Amy's parents. When he came back into the cabin, he told the children it was time to go. The roads they would travel on were safe to drive.

"But we're having so much fun!" Amy said.

Mr. Rooney smiled. "You can come back and visit anytime."

The children cheered.

Everyone worked together to get the dogs settled in the back of the van. Toby was the last to leave.

Elliot clipped on the dog's leash and started for the door. Mr. Rooney took the leash from him. "That's okay, Elliot," Mr. Rooney said. "I already spoke to Sam and Tina. Toby will be staying with me from now on."

"Really?"

Mr. Rooney nodded. "I forgot how much I missed having a dog. After Quincy died, I thought I'd never have a place in my heart for another animal." He stroked Toby's head. "But Toby and I seem to get along."

Elliot smiled. He knew that Toby would have a good home with Mr.

Rooney. He crouched and looked into the dog's dark-brown eyes. "Goodbye, Toby," he said. "Next time I come, I'll bring you a special treat."

When the van pulled up to the shelter, there was a car already in the parking lot. It had a Maine license plate. A tall man and two children, a girl and a boy, got out. The man shook Sam's hand. "My name is Thomas Cardozo," he said. "And this is Maddie and Atticus."

"Yes," Sam said. "You called earlier to say you were dropping by."

"That's right," said Mr. Cardozo. "We're on our way home from a family vacation. When we stopped in a restaurant in town to wait out the storm, the waitress told us about your shelter. We looked up your website and—"

"We saw a photo of the new puppies!" Maddie exclaimed. "We *really* want to adopt one."

"Have you had any experience with taking care of puppies?" Sam asked.

"Oh yes," said Atticus. "We helped take care of a dog last summer."

"He was always getting into trouble," Maddie said. "But we miss him."

"I told the kids we could adopt a puppy when we got home," their father said. "But when we saw the puppies on the website, we thought we'd stop in."

"First things first," Sam said. "We have to get the dogs settled. Then you can pick a puppy, and we'll do the paperwork."

Everybody pitched in, and soon the dogs were back inside the shelter.

Maddie peered into the cage holding the litter of puppies. "That's a cute one,"

she said. She pointed straight to Penny.

"What do you think, Atticus?"

Atticus nodded. "I like her."

•YOUR NEW PUPPY•

It's an exciting day when you bring a puppy into your home. But wait! Are you prepared?

🐾 A cozy bed inside a crate provides a safe place for the puppy to sleep when you're not around.

- Your puppy will also need a collar, a leash, and an ID tag that has your address and telephone number on it.

- Puppies need special food so they grow strong.

- Puppies love to play, so you'll need lots of toys.

- Find a vet and schedule a visit right away. A healthy puppy is a happy puppy.

- Set up a schedule. Who will feed the puppy? When will she eat? Who will house-train her? When will she go outside? You will need to discuss these questions with your family. It's a good idea to make a chart that lists who is responsible for what.

And most of all, a puppy needs . . . YOU!

Amy's bottom lip began to quiver. She blinked back tears.

Sam took Penny from the cage.

Amy's tears spilled over.

Maddie reached for the puppy.

"I'm sorry," Sam said. "This one is already taken."

"It is?" Maddie said.

"It is?" Amy said.

Sam nodded. "But you can choose any of the others."

Maddie and Atticus picked the puppy with the splotch over its eye. They went to wait in the back office for Sam.

"So who is adopting Penny?" Amy asked. Her voice wobbled.

Sam placed the puppy in her arms. "You are," he said. "I spoke to your parents earlier. I told them how responsible you were with the dogs. They agreed to let you have Penny. Unless you'd like a different one?"

"No!" Amy cried. "Penny is the only dog for me." She hugged her new pet, and the puppy nibbled her finger.

"Yay!" Kyung said. "Now we both have dogs."

Amy turned to Elliot. "Why don't you adopt a puppy?" she asked. "Then our puppies could play together when we hang out."

"We're going to hang out?" he said.

"Of course," Amy said. "We're friends now. Didn't you know?"

Elliot hadn't known. But he was glad to have Amy and Kyung as friends.

Bye!

BE A VOLUNTEER!

There are many ways you can help animals.
Here are just a few ideas to get you started.

Raise money for organizations
that aid animals, such as rescue
centers and pet shelters.
Organize a bake sale or a yard
sale and donate the money to
your favorite animal charity.

Animal hospitals, vets, and
pet shelters often need help
caring for animals. You and
a parent or guardian can
volunteer to clean out dirty
cages, feed the animals, or
take dogs for walks.

Organize a pet-food drive.
Shelters and rescue centers
need food to feed all the
animals they care for.

"So what about getting a dog?" Kyung said.

Elliot shook his head. "I don't think so." He looked around at the animals in their cages and thought of Toby. "So many of the dogs here don't have homes yet. I'm going to come to the shelter and spend time with them." He opened his arms wide. "That way they'll *all* be my dogs!"

"Yay!" cried Kyung. "I'll come too."

"Count me in," Amy said.

Sam grinned. "It looks like Adopt-Your-BFF just got three new volunteers."

animal planet™

Farm Friends Escape!

Gail Herman
Illustrated by Bryan Langdo

Contents

• ALL IN THE FAMILY •

A family farm is one that has been run by the same family—not a company— for many years.

Welcome to the Farm

The sun was shining. The morning was warm. It felt like summer. Eleven-year-old Sarah Turner giggled. Of course it felt like summer. It *was* summer! It was July. From the back seat of the car, she looked out the window. She couldn't stop smiling!

Sarah's mother was driving. "You know, Sarah," she said, "you'll be at the farm for weeks. You won't see us for a while."

"Yes," Sarah's father added. He glanced at his smiling daughter. "Try not to miss us *too* much."

"Oh, I'll miss you guys," Sarah said. "I always do. But I'm excited!" She rolled down the window. The breeze blew her ponytail. And she smiled even wider.

Sarah spent summers with her grandparents. They owned a small farm in Massachusetts. Sarah loved it there. *Wait!* Sarah thought. *I'll make a list of the things I like about the farm.* She flipped open a notebook to a blank page. She always kept a notebook nearby. She liked to organize her thoughts. Sarah wrote:

FARM LIKES
1. Animals
2. Fresh fruit

The farm had all kinds of animals. And Sarah liked each and every one.

Sarah liked the vegetables too—but not as much as the strawberries and blueberries.

Oh! What about people? she thought. She started another list.

FARM LOVES
1. Grandma Rose and Grandpa Tom
2. Luke (when he's not joking around)

Luke was Sarah's cousin. He spent summers at the farm too.

SWEET BERRIES

Some farms let people come and pick their own fruits and vegetables. Visitors can see how food grows. They can learn about what it's like to live on a farm.

Sarah loved Luke—most of the time. They were the same age. And, like Sarah, he was an only child. In a way, they grew up together during the summers with their grandparents.

Sarah turned the notebook page.

THINGS I DON'T LIKE ABOUT
THE FARM
1. Leaving

Sarah sighed. That wasn't entirely true. Sarah's family lived in Maine. Luke's family lived in New York. After leaving the farm, both families always drove straight to a beach cottage to spend a week together. Sarah had fun being by the ocean with Luke, her parents, and her aunt and uncle. But it

MANY EARS

Most of the corn farmers grow does not end up on the dinner table. Instead, a lot is used to feed cows and other animals such as chickens. Some is turned into cooking oil. Some is used to make drinks and dessert. Some is even turned into fuel to make cars go.

Chickens scratch the ground with their feet to find food.

wasn't the same as being at the farm.

After driving a few hours, they turned down a dirt road. "There it is!" Sarah cried suddenly. "The farm!"

Pretty rosebushes grew next to the white house. The huge red barn stood close by. Fields and meadows spread out behind the barn. A duck pond sparkled in the sun.

Sarah's mom pulled into the driveway. Grandma Rose flung open the front door. "Tom!" she called. "They're here!"

Sarah jumped out of the car. "Grandma! I'm almost as tall as you."

When her grandfather walked over, Sarah hugged them both tightly. They smelled of grass and fresh air. Sarah's grandparents dressed alike too,

MILKIN' IT!

Farmers milk their cows two times a day. On larger dairy farms, machines gently take the milk from the cows. Happy cows make more milk, so farmers take good care of their cows.

with matching jeans and boots. But
Grandpa Tom was bald and serious-
looking. And Grandma Rose had a
long, gray braid and a cheerful grin.

Everyone hugged some more and
talked at the same time. Then another
car pulled up.

"It's Luke! Yay!" cried Sarah. She ran
up to the car. Luke grinned through the

window. He had his summer haircut—not too long, not too short. "Open the door for me!" he shouted. He waved his hands full of candy bars.

"Okay!" Sarah tugged on the handle. It was covered in something mushy and brown. "Ugh." She jumped away. "What *is* that?"

Luke opened the door. "Peanut butter!" He laughed and handed Sarah a napkin. "Got you! Didn't I?"

A practical joke. And before he even got *out* of the car. Sarah groaned. "You are not funny, Luke!"

"Am too."

"No fighting," Grandpa Tom said sternly. "You two have to get along this summer."

A-MAZE-ING!

Some farmers use hay bales to create a fun game. They place the bales in a pattern called a maze. People have to find their way to the center and back out again. Hay mazes are popular at Halloween.

Luke and Sarah stopped fussing. Grandma Rose came over. Dan, the farmhand, joined them too.

"Hi, Dan!" said Luke and Sarah. Dan gave them big smiles. He was nice, but quiet.

"Dan will be busy in the fields all summer," Grandpa Tom went on. "We're starting a new crop. So he won't be running the petting zoo." He looked at Sarah and Luke. "You will be. Together."

The cousins gasped. They were going to be in charge!

Teamwork

After lunch Luke and Sarah said a quick goodbye to their parents. They were eager to go see the animals in the barn. The only animal they'd seen so far was the old farm dog, Duncan.

"Can we go to the barn now?" Luke asked Grandma Rose excitedly.

"Yup. Let's go!" Grandma Rose answered. "I have a lot to tell you about the animals."

Sarah grabbed her notebook. Luke

grabbed a few peanut butter twists.
Then they followed Grandma Rose into
the barn.

Animal stalls and pens lined the
sides of the barn. The animals were
quiet.

"It's their naptime," Sarah whispered.

"That's right," said Grandma Rose.
"In the heat of the day, they rest."

Luke crept close to Sarah. "Mooooo!"
he said loudly. She jumped. Some
animals snorted and bleated. Then they
quieted down.

"Luke, you know better," Grandma
Rose said in a stern voice. But she
followed it with a wink.

Sarah frowned.

Why can't Sarah relax? Luke

wondered. *Even a little bit?*

"We have some babies," Grandma Rose announced. "They are—"

"So cute!" Sarah interrupted. She and Luke rushed to the pigpen.

The tiny piglets snuffled their noses. They stayed close to their mother under the straw.

"Slow down," Grandma Rose warned. "They can't see very well. And don't pick them up. They don't like that."

"Right. Okay," Luke said, disappointed. He glanced at Sarah. She was busy scribbling notes. She kept writing as Grandma Rose went over chores and animal care.

Grandma Rose stopped by each group of animals: cows, goats, sheep, chickens, rabbits. She pointed to one rabbit. "We think Snuffles is having babies soon," she said. She talked about early feedings and late feedings. Checking hooves for rocks and twigs. Grooming and brushing.

PILE O' PIGLETS
A pig can have 12 babies, and sometimes even more! Newborn piglets drink milk from their mother, or nurse, once or twice an hour.

Luke half-listened. *Sarah will write down all the information*, he thought.

Suddenly, he scooped up a fluffy hen. He examined her carefully. "Hey, I just read about chickens!" he exclaimed. "One side always has more feathers than the other."

"Really?" Sarah looked at the hen closely. "Which side?" She held her pen ready to write.

"The outside."

Sarah laughed. *Wow! So she's got a sense of humor after all!* Luke thought. He grinned back.

Just then Grandpa Tom poked his head in. "Time for work," he announced.

"With the animals?" Luke asked.

"First comes cleaning, raking, and painting. The petting zoo needs to be ready."

All that week and the next, Luke and Sarah worked on the petting zoo. They mended the fence around the pen. They raked and tidied. They painted the shelter. Then they filled it with hay and bedding.

Each day, they brought animals from the barn to visit the zoo. Later, they returned them to the barn. The goats nosed around, curious. The sheep stuck close together. Luke studied how the animals acted. Sarah watched them too. The cousins would have to choose the right animals to be part of the zoo. Each animal had to have a friendly and playful personality, so they'd get along with the children.

I'd be great in a petting zoo, Luke decided. He wasn't so sure about Sarah. She was *so* serious. They were completing morning chores in the barn and Sarah was checking her to-do list. "Organize feed bags," she read out loud. Then she called to Luke, "The quickest way to finish a job is to do it right the first time."

"Nope!" Luke answered. "The quickest way to finish a job is to move fast!" He raced across the pen, lifting four bags of chicken feed at once.

Oof! He tripped over his own feet. The bags tumbled to the ground. Feed scattered across the floor. Hens and

LEFTOVERS

Pigs eat everything: fruits and vegetables, grains and meat. They even like to eat bugs and a little bit of dirt.

Farm Fact

OINK! OINK!

Pigs talk to one another. All those grunts, oinks, and squeals mean something.

On a farm, everyone pitches in. On many farms, kids do chores before and after school, including feeding animals and gathering eggs.

chicks raced over to gobble it up.

"Hey!" he called to Sarah. "You can cross 'feed the chickens' off the list."

Then he had another idea. He swept up the feed. The chickens clucked around him. "Luke is awesome," he said, sprinkling a few pellets. Bit by bit, he fed the chickens more pellets. Each time, he'd say, "Luke is awesome." After a while, when he'd say, "Luke is awesome," they'd come running.

"Pretty great trick, huh?" He smiled.

Sarah wasn't paying attention. She was busy filling water bowls with the hose.

Luke sighed. He couldn't complain about Sarah too much, though. She was a hard worker. "Let's take some animals to the petting zoo," he told her.

Just as Grandma Rose had taught them, they gently nudged the goats from the barn.

Suddenly, Sarah stopped. She pointed at the ground. "Candy wrappers!" She glared at Luke. "You were taking snack breaks? While I was busy working? And you littered!"

"No! I did not!" Luke sputtered.

"Who else eats peanut butter twists?" she cried.

Luke was about to answer, but the goats had trotted off. Now they were munching on Grandpa Tom's prized rosebushes. "Your fault!" shouted Luke as he and Sarah raced over.

"No! Your fault!" Sarah shouted back.

GET OFF MY BAA-CK

Goats love to climb. They even climb on other animals!

Farm Fact

SELF-SERVICE

Goats are very smart and know how to get what they want. Scientists have taught them to solve puzzles to get their food.

Like donkeys, goats graze. This means they eat grass and other types of plants.

They pulled the goats away. But only one rose was left on each bush. Luke groaned. They were in trouble already. And they hadn't even opened the petting zoo yet.

Petting Zoo—Open!

After weeks of preparing, it was opening day. Sarah and Luke had chosen the animals for the petting zoo: two small goats named Agnes and Heidi, Daisy the cow, two bunnies named Cuddles and Snuffles, chickens Grace and May, and sheep Willy, Woolly, and Mo. But there was still a lot to do.

The cousins woke up to pouring rain

at sunrise. Luke grumbled. Sarah was too excited to care.

"The weather will clear up," Grandma Rose promised.

So Sarah and Luke pulled on their raincoats and went out to the zoo. They filled feed machines. They checked soap dispensers. Visitors would have to wash their hands at the gate before they entered the zoo and as they left. This was so they and the animals wouldn't trade germs.

The cousins filled the animals' water bowls. They cleared animal droppings. They made sure the animals had fresh hay. Sarah checked each chore off her list. "Time to get the animals, then put out the sign!" she said finally.

Luke wanted to put the sign out first—*then* get the animals. Of course, Sarah disagreed. But she didn't want to argue. Not today! So they went to get the sign.

The big sign read "Petting Zoo—Open" on the front. And it had a flip board in one corner. When it was lifted, the sign read "Closed." It was a good idea, Sarah thought. But the board flapped open and shut. This made it hard for them to carry the heavy sign to the entrance of the farm.

"Move faster, Luke!" Sarah huffed. She didn't think she could hold on. Thankfully, Luke picked up speed.

Thud! They dropped the sign in the

CUDDLE CORNER

Taking care of animals is a lot of work. They need food. They need water. They need a place to live that is clean, safe, and comfortable. In the winter, they need to stay warm. In the summer, they need to stay cool.

A veterinarian looks after the animals when they are sick. Animals get doctor visits when they are healthy too, just like children. On a family farm, there's plenty of work for everyone.

Farm Fact

HEAT LAMP

Baby chicks get cold very easily, and need heat lamps to stay warm.

Cows can be taught to walk on a leash.

Rabbits enjoy treats in addition to their regular food.

Lambs and sheep are happiest in groups.

Baby chicks need water, food, and a warm coop.

mud by the road. Luke set it upright.

Sarah caught her breath. "Where should we put it?"

"It's fine right here," said Luke.

"No. It needs to be in a better spot. More to the left."

"No, it doesn't."

"Yes, it does. People will see it better."

Luke ran a hand over his hair. "You know where you want it. Why did you ask me?"

"What's your problem?"

"I think you came out earlier and decided on your own."

"I did not!"

"Yes, you did! Look!" He pointed to smudges in the mud. Footprints.

Those prints were way too big to

SHOW ME

At a fair, kids can show off the animals they raised themselves. The judges look to see if the animals have been well cared for. They judge how healthy the animals look. Then they pick the winners.

be hers. Sarah was about to say so.
But then she spied someone by the
trees. She couldn't make out the figure.
Whoever it was had been there before.
She thought she'd seen someone a few

times, lurking near the farm. Hiding.

She had a thought. "I bet those
footprints are Grandma's or Grandpa's.
They're probably sneaking around,
checking on us," she said.

"Hmm," Luke said thoughtfully.
"You may be right. I've felt like someone

was watching us too. They probably want to make sure we're working—and not fighting."

Luke and Sarah looked at each other and nodded. Luke moved the sign to the left. And together, they pushed the sign pole into the ground.

Next, they hurried to the barn. By now, Sarah's excitement had turned into nervousness. And it seemed she had passed on her nervous feelings to the animals. The goats wouldn't stay still. Agnes raced up the ladder to the hayloft. And when Sarah followed, Agnes raced back down. Heidi stuck her head in a bucket and couldn't get it out. Sarah pulled the bucket off. Then Snuffles and Cuddles wouldn't come out

PETTING ZOO HOW-TO

It's fun to pet the animals at a petting zoo. Be sure to close the gate behind you, so they don't run away. Feed them only food the farmer puts out. Other food may make them sick.

Farm Fact

CLEANUP TIME

Be sure to wash your hands when you leave a petting zoo. Sometimes animals have germs that are harmful to people.

of the rabbit hutch.

"Maybe this will work." Luke wrinkled his nose and hopped like a bunny. "Cuddles. Snuffles. Look!" he said. He jumped around, knocking over a water bowl. He went to fill it again— then he stopped short. "Sarah! I see somebody by the trees. It's not Grandma or Grandpa."

Sarah hurried over. "Is it Dan?"

"No!" Luke pointed to a figure. "It's a kid."

"Do you mean a boy or girl or baby goat?" Sarah asked.

"A boy. And he's watching us."

Sarah's eyes widened. "He must have left the footprints."

"And the candy wrappers," Luke

added. He raced out of the petting zoo toward the kid. But the boy saw him coming. He turned and fled. Luke walked back, shrugging. "He just disappeared."

"It's just as well," Sarah said. She shook away thoughts of the suspicious boy. "Let's round up the animals. Here come Grandma and Grandpa to see if we're ready. It's time to open. We have a petting zoo to run."

Petting Zoo Escape

The zoo had been open for more than an hour. They hadn't had one visitor. Luke felt tired already. Just getting Agnes and Heidi into the pen had been difficult. The goats hated the rain. Maybe the weather was keeping people away too. But now the sun shone through the clouds. And still the cousins waited.

THE SCOOP ON POOP

Every day, farmers have to take away all the poop their animals make. They save it to fertilize the soil, or make it richer. But first, they have to compost it. That means letting bacteria break it down into mush. Bacteria are tiny living things that can help or hurt animals and people.

The first step for turning poop into compost is to mix the poop with plant matter, such as grass clippings, leaves, or used hay. Then farmers let compost sit for a few months. Finally, they spread the compost on the soil to help the plants grow.

Farm Fact

MEADOW MUFFIN

NAME GAME
There are lots of words for poop: manure, dung, muck, cow patty, meadow muffin, road apple, and droppings.

Clearing a place where a farm animal lives, such as a horse's stall, is called "mucking out."

Where is everybody? Luke wondered. Then he had a sudden thought. *The sign! The flip board must say the zoo is closed!*

He raced down the driveway. He was right. He flipped the sign to "Petting Zoo—Open."

Not much later, they had their first visitors: three-year-old twin boys with their parents. The boys washed their hands. They made bags of feed. They were gentle with the animals. *Easy peasy,* thought Luke.

But it was not as easy as he thought. Luke had to stop one little girl from eating goat droppings. She thought they were berries. Then he caught a little boy pulling Daisy's tail. Still, it was a lot of fun. Luke laughed as Agnes followed the children around. Those goats were always so curious, always watching people come and go.

"Luke!" Sarah was hurrying over as he filled the feed machine. "He's here!" she hissed. Immediately, Luke knew whom she meant—the suspicious boy.

"Go over to him!" Luke said. "I'll come when I'm finished."

"Me?" Sarah squeaked. Then she took a deep breath and rushed out of the pen. But a family of six was coming in at the same time. For a moment, they blocked the entrance. Sarah was stuck in the crowd. And then the boy was gone.

"It's okay," Luke told her. "That wasn't your fault. But we should tell Grandma and Grandpa. That boy is strange."

Sarah agreed.

But there were more visitors and more chores. Later, there was the afternoon feeding. Then they returned the animals to the barn and bathed some of them. By dinner, the cousins were too tired to talk. As they got ready for bed, Sarah said sleepily, "I'll write up a 'suspicious boy' list in the morning."

Early the next day, Luke and Sarah brought the animals to the petting zoo. Then the cousins sat down for breakfast with their grandparents.

"We have something to tell you," Luke said. "We've seen—" He paused. "Animals!"

FILL HER UP

What a cow eats affects how much milk she makes and even how the milk tastes. If a cow eats only grass, she can make about 50 glasses of milk a day. If she also eats some corn, hay, and other foods, she can make twice as much milk.

"Of course we've seen animals!"
Sarah said, annoyed. "We're on a farm.
Stop joking around."

"No!" Luke gripped her arm. "Look!"
He pointed to the window. Everyone
stared outside.

Daisy was running past. Behind her, Agnes and Heidi trotted down the driveway.

The cousins and their grandparents jumped to their feet. The petting zoo animals had escaped!

On the Case

Grandma Rose and Grandpa Tom rushed down the driveway. Luke and Sarah raced to the pen. They hoped some animals had stayed behind. But the petting zoo was empty. No rabbits. No sheep. Not even one chicken.

"What are we going to do?" Sarah cried. Her voice rose with worry.

"Come on!" Luke grabbed her hand. They ran to their grandparents, staring down the empty road.

AN APPLE A DAY

There are more than 7,500 kinds of apples. Apples can be red, green, or yellow. Some are sweet and some are sour. Some are hard and crisp, some are soft. Some taste best right from the tree. Others taste better when you cook them.

Grandma Rose checked her watch. "We have to make our morning deliveries," she said to Grandpa Tom. Each morning, they drove the farm truck to local restaurants and grocery stores to deliver fruits and vegetables.

"But we need to find the animals first," said Grandpa Tom.

Luke and Sarah exchanged looks. Their grandparents had a business to run. Sarah felt she and Luke could handle it on their own. "You can go," she told them. "We can take care of the animals."

"Definitely!" Luke agreed.

Grandpa shook his head no. He didn't say anything. Maybe he thought they had left the zoo's gate open.

But Luke was already steering

them toward the truck. "We know the animals, Grandpa. The animals know us. We can do it!"

"Tom." Grandma Rose touched his arm. "Today is the first day we deliver to that big supermarket. The truck is already loaded. We really shouldn't be late." She smiled at the cousins. "I trust Luke and Sarah."

After more discussion, Grandpa Tom agreed. Grandma Rose would make calls while he drove. She'd let neighbors know to look out for the animals. "And Dan is already on his way here," she said. "He will help."

"We'll make our deliveries quickly," Grandpa said.

Seconds later, the truck roared off.

Sarah's heart raced. Their grandparents were gone. All of a sudden, she didn't feel so sure about things. "Now what?" she asked.

"We act fast!" said Luke. "Let's search around the petting zoo again."

The empty pen seemed strange, Sarah thought. And a little spooky. Was that Cuddles in the corner? She rushed closer. No—it wasn't the rabbit. It was only leaves.

"How did they escape?" Luke was puzzled. "We need to look for clues. Did you stack the feed buckets last night?" Luke asked.

"Yes."

"Well, look. They're scattered around now."

ROADSIDE ATTRACTION

Some farmers sell their extra fruits and vegetables in a farm stand. That's a little store on the side of the road. Everything in the farm stand is super fresh.

STRAWBERRIES

Sweet and delicious, these berries grow low to the ground. They are ripe in the spring.

WATERMELONS

This summer favorite grows on a vine. The heavy fruit rests on the ground.

EGGPLANTS

Sun and warm weather help this vegetable grow.

TOMATOES

These were first grown in South America. Now people all over the world love them.

"Hmm. And those crates are in different spots too." Sarah pointed out two crates, overturned by the gate. "Looks like somebody snuck in and messed around. Do you think it's that boy?"

She gazed toward the trees. She almost expected the boy to be there, lurking as before. Then she noticed something on the ground.

"Hey!" she exclaimed. "Footprints!" In the mud, between the zoo and trees, were more prints. These were clear and easy to see.

"Sneaker prints!" said Luke.

It had to be that kid!

Runaway Roundup

How could that boy do *this?* Luke wondered. He understood about pranks and practical jokes. He figured the boy might think this would be funny. But it put the animals in danger. He and Sarah had to find them.

"Where would they go?" Luke asked.

Sarah thought out loud. "The sheep and goats will stay in groups. That should make it easier."

"Okay then." Luke tapped his foot impatiently. "Let's get going. It's better if we split up."

They divided responsibilities. Luke headed to the small wooded area. He'd stay near the farm, in case any animals came back. This had to work out!

Sarah hopped on a bike to search the neighborhood. *Sheep,* she thought. *Where would they go? They couldn't have gone too far. What was close by?*

Last summer she and Luke had spent days searching a field for four-leaf clover. That field was just down the road. She knew sheep loved clover. The field would be perfect for grazing. Sarah pedaled away.

In no time, the field came into view. *Yes!* Sarah pumped her fist. Three fluffy shapes were in the far corner— Willy, Woolly, and Mo. They bent their heads and grazed.

"Yay!" Sarah shouted. In the quiet of the morning, her cry rang out loudly. The sheep twitched, startled. Sheep have excellent hearing, Sarah knew. She shouldn't scare them. They might take off again.

Sarah did not move. After a few moments, the sheep went back to grazing. She inched forward quietly. Bit by bit, she drew closer.

LIVING LAWNMOWERS

Sheep like to graze on tasty grasses. They will move from area to area as they eat. Sheep like to stay together in groups to graze. When one sheep heads to a new area, the others follow.

Wide-set eyes allow sheep to see things behind them without turning their heads.

SNACK TIME!

In addition to grass, sheep munch on other plants in the pasture. Favorites include clover and sunflowers.

Finally, Sarah stood next to them. She scratched their ears and smiled.

But how could she bring them back to the farm? They wouldn't want to go. Not with all this clover to eat!

NO WAY!

A flock will follow a leader. But a single lamb may be stubborn.

She tried pushing and prodding the sheep. First Willy, then Woolly, then Mo. *Just one*, she thought. If one got moving, the other two would follow. But Sarah was out of luck. Not one sheep budged.

What else could she do? Who could help? She had an idea: *Duncan! He is a herding dog, after all.*

In a flash, Sarah rode home. She brought Duncan back. Excited to be outside, he ran next to the bike. *He's almost like a puppy again,* Sarah thought.

Then Duncan saw the sheep. "Go on, boy," Sarah said. "Let's take them home."

Immediately, Duncan went into action. He nosed the sheep away from the field and ran ahead to show them the way. Then he doubled back to prod them. Again and again, he urged them forward. Sarah rode next to them so they wouldn't veer off path. It took awhile. But Sarah and Duncan herded the sheep right back into the petting zoo.

In the distance, Sarah saw Luke. He was searching around the trees. "I got the sheep!" she called.

"Good! Try for the goats," he shouted back to her.

"If you were a goat, where would you go?" she asked Duncan. The dog cocked his head, as if he were thinking. "You'd like to jump and climb, so . . ." Sarah suddenly snapped her fingers.

"What about a playground?"

She and Luke had played at the elementary school playground many times. The goats might have gone in that direction. The school was in the opposite direction from the clover field. She took a deep breath. It would be a long bike ride.

Beep! Beep! Dan pulled into the driveway in his pickup truck just then. Sarah ran over and explained everything.

"Hop in!" said Dan.

Sarah and Duncan jumped into the truck. As Dan drove, Sarah looked all around, in case the goats were on the road. Minutes later, they reached the school. Dan swung around the building and parked at the edge of the playground.

"They're here!" Sarah cried.

Two towers stood at either end of a giant climbing structure. A bridge connected them. *Maaa. Maaa.* Agnes was trotting across the bridge. *Clop, clop.* Sarah almost laughed. Maybe there was a troll underneath, like in "The Three Billy Goats Gruff."

Heidi stepped onto the bottom of a seesaw. She started up the board. As she skipped past the middle, the other side went down. She skipped even faster. At the end, she turned around to do it all over again.

Sarah, Dan, and Duncan hopped out of the truck. "Duncan!" Sarah called. "Herding time!"

BORDER PATROL

Border collies control sheep using
a special look called "the eye."
They lower their head and stare at
the sheep to make them move.

Farm Fact

ALL ACTION

Border collies need lots of things to do. They have tons of energy and like to play.

For some dog breeds, herding is a natural skill. In a family home, a herder may nudge a family member toward the dog food dish.

But Duncan just lay in the shade, panting. The poor old dog was hot and tired. He'd be no help now. Sarah watched Agnes. Maybe she and Dan could catch Agnes first. The goat was skidding down a slide. Sarah moved closer. Dan moved closer. But Agnes scampered away quickly. She darted around the swings. She leaped over benches. She moved so fast, they didn't have a chance to grab her.

Maybe Heidi, Sarah thought.

But Heidi was scooting up the climbing mountain now. When Sarah reached for her, she jumped off and raced away.

"We'll never get them!" Sarah groaned.

"I may have something we can use to pen them in," Dan said quietly. "I think I have some fencing." He reached under a tarp in the back of the truck. Then he took out two mesh rolls. He and Sarah unrolled them, then waited. Minutes later, both goats stopped under the bridge to chew on a pile of twigs.

Sarah cried, "Now!"

Working at top speed, she and Dan set up the fences around the towers. The goats were trapped.

"Oh, Agnes," Sarah said, reaching in to hug her close. "You silly thing." She led Agnes onto the truck, and Dan got Heidi.

"Duncan!" Sarah called. "Home!" The dog raced over. "*Now* he's running." Sarah laughed.

Dan drove to the farm, and they took the goats into the petting zoo. The sheep were in the shelter, and now Agnes and Heidi were too. The animals all grew quiet, eating and resting after their big adventure.

Dan headed off to continue the search. Sarah sighed and looked around. She didn't see Luke anywhere.

"*Woof!*" Duncan herded Sarah into the house. "I know, I know," she said. "You want to eat too!"

She'd fed Duncan, then went to go find Luke. Sarah crossed her fingers for good luck. She only hoped Luke and the other animals were okay.

Follow the Footprints

Luke, meanwhile, had found two sets of animal prints in the mud. Following them, he stepped into the wooded area behind the barn. He bent to examine the prints. One set looked like a cow's hooves. *Daisy,* he thought. The other set looked like arrows. Chicken prints— Grace and May.

Daisy first, Luke decided. He tracked the hoofprints around the trees. When

WALK THIS WAY

HOOVES

Many farm animals walk on hooves. A hoof is a hard covering at the end of a foot. Hooves are made of keratin, the same stuff as your fingernails.

HORSE

TWO-PART HOOVES

Some animal hooves have two parts. Pigs, goats, sheep, and cows have two-part hooves.

GOAT

WEBBED FEET

Ducks and geese have extra skin between their toes, called webbing. Webbed feet act like paddles. They make ducks and geese good swimmers.

GOOSE

PADDED FEET

CAT

Dogs, cats, and rabbits all have soft pads on their feet. The pads help them run fast and land softly.

the dirt and tracks ended, Luke looked around. He was at the edge of a meadow. Daisy was there, happily munching on grass. She looked up and saw him. Then she went back to grazing.

"Daisy, Daisy," Luke said softly. He just wanted to grab onto her quickly. But he held himself back. He didn't want to spook her.

"How are you doing, Daisy?" Luke kept talking in a soothing voice. Slowly, he edged closer. Finally, he took hold of her collar. *Got you!* he thought. Still moving slowly, he led her home.

Back at the pen, Luke peered into the shelter. The goats and sheep were inside. Immediately, Luke felt better. He didn't see Sarah. But that was okay.

They were making progress. There were just the chickens and rabbits left. And he had an idea where the chickens had gone.

He passed a feed bucket, then stopped. Why hadn't he thought of this earlier? They could use food to get the animals home! He grabbed the bucket. He hurried back to follow the chicken prints.

Luke followed the trail for a few feet. But then the prints stopped. They didn't go left or right. They just disappeared. How could that be?

"Okay," he said out loud. "Chickens can't just disappear."

Why hadn't he listened more closely when Grandma Rose had talked about animal behavior? Then he remembered

one important fact. Chickens can fly!
At least a bit. So he gazed up into a
tree close by. There, on a low branch,
sat Grace and May. *Cluck! Cluck!* They
seemed happy. And in no hurry to leave.

"Luke is awesome," Luke called
softly. He tossed some feed under the
branch. Still clucking, they hopped
right off.

"Luke is awesome!" Luke repeated,
starting back to the farm. He left a trail
of feed. The chickens followed behind,
pecking at the food. Finally, they
reached the pen. "Whew!" Luke sighed.
He had just run out of feed.

"Luke!" Sarah called, hurrying into
the pen. "I was just feeding Duncan in
the house." Then she grinned. "You got

Daisy and the chickens!" She held up her hand for a high five. "Awesome!"

Luke raised his hand too. But at the word "awesome," the chickens rose in the air. They squawked and flapped their wings, looking for food. Luke and Sarah slapped away the feathers.

"Forget it, Sarah," said Luke, laughing. Then he turned serious. "Now let's find those rabbits."

✿ ✿ ✿

A Double Surprise

Sarah grabbed carrots for rabbit bait. "Let's search by the duck pond, Luke," she said.

Together, they walked toward a bunch of trees. Just a few steps in, they found Cuddles snuggled on the ground by a tree trunk. The poor rabbit was shivering. His ears were flat. He was scared. Sarah crouched closer. "Cuddles," she whispered, "we're here. It's okay." She held out a carrot.

BUNNY BABIES

Rabbits are born with their eyes closed and without fur. They have some fur by the time they are 7 days old. Their eyes open after about 10 or 11 days.

These bunnies will stay in the nest for about a month. Then they can hop off on their own.

Farm Fact

LEGGING IT

Rabbits have really strong back legs. This helps them run fast. They can also kick with their back legs to protect themselves.

He sniffed it, nibbled, and relaxed as Sarah petted him.

"Okay, now where's Snuffles?" Luke asked. Cuddles began to hop down a path. "Maybe he knows!" Sarah said.

The cousins started along the trail behind him. They edged around a bend. Then they stopped short. Luke gasped.

"It's you!" Sarah exclaimed.

The suspicious boy was standing in the middle of the path. Up close, Sarah could see he had freckles and dark-brown eyes. The boy faced them, crossing his arms. *It's like he's guarding something,* Sarah thought. *He won't let us pass.*

Behind the boy, a small furry creature dug under leaves. "It's Snuffles! He's got Snuffles!" Sarah cried.

Luke quickly scooped up Cuddles and held him tight.

"I have a name," the boy said. "It's Pete."

"Okay, Pete," said Luke angrily. "We want our rabbit back!"

"No!" Pete replied.

Sarah's heart sank. What would they do now? Call their grandparents?

"You can't move her," Pete went on. "I think she's about to have babies."

"Our grandma already *told* us Snuffles was having babies," Luke replied. "But what makes *you* the rabbit expert? How do you know it's about to happen *now*?"

Pete blushed. "Well, I've always wanted a pet rabbit. So I've done a ton

PETS ON A FARM

BARN BUDDY

Cats are welcome on a farm. They keep mice away from the other animals' food.

LITTLE PIGGIES

Guinea pigs like to live with other guinea pigs. When they are happy, they purr, just like a cat.

HEE-HAW

Donkeys are strong and smart. They like to live in groups. If there are no other donkeys around, they will make friends with goats.

of reading." He looked down at Snuffles. "She's trying to build a nest. See?"

Snuffles was busy collecting grass

and twigs. She even pulled out some of her fur, using her teeth. She added the fur to the pile. Then she burrowed under it all.

"Well, maybe you're right," Sarah said to Pete. "But what should we do?"

"We could help," Pete said quietly. "Do you have a nest box?"

"Yes!" said Sarah. "We could use it to carry her back to the farm."

"Good idea," Luke agreed. "Snuffles and her babies will be safer there."

Sarah raced to the barn. She hurried back with the box. Then she and Luke carefully lifted Snuffles with the grass, twigs, and fur into the nest box. Luke carried the box. Sarah carried Cuddles. She told Luke when to watch out for rocks on the path. And Pete trailed behind.

Back at the barn, the cousins placed the box in the rabbit hutch. The babies came in minutes. Sarah and Luke looked at the babies. There were five altogether. They were tiny, without any fur. Snuffles covered them with her own fur, like a blanket.

"We got her back just in time," Sarah whispered.

"Good job, Snuffles," Luke said softly.

All at once, Sarah realized Pete hadn't come into the barn. He was waiting outside.

"Hey, thanks for your help," Luke told him as they stepped through the doors. "But we have to ask you something. Why have you been watching us?"

Pete looked down, embarrassed. "Well, I love all animals. Not just rabbits. That's why I've been hanging around here."

"You should have just come to the petting zoo!" Sarah exclaimed.

"That's the crazy thing," Pete said in a low voice. "I love animals. But I'm scared of them. I don't want to get too close." He looked at the cousins nervously. "I know it's lame. But watching you take care of the animals— it's the closest I've come to petting one."

Sarah and Luke burst out laughing.

"Go ahead and laugh," Pete said miserably. "I know it's ridiculous."

"No, that's not it," Sarah said. "I'm afraid of lots of things. But we thought you were up to something. You know, something suspicious."

"So *you* didn't let the animals out?" Luke asked.

Pete shook his head. "I'd never do that."

"Well, that takes care of one mystery," Sarah said.

"Yeah, and it leaves a bigger one," Luke added.

How did the animals escape?

CHAPTER 9

Mystery Solved

After Pete went home, the animals came out of the petting zoo shelter. They all seemed rested. Finally able to relax, Luke and Sarah sat in a corner watching them.

"Look at Agnes!" Luke whispered curiously. The cousins watched in amazement.

The small goat pushed a crate to a feeding machine. Then she stood on the crate to reach a knob on the machine.

She took the knob in her mouth. Then she turned it. Feed poured out of the chute. The other animals trotted over.

The cousins looked at each other, amazed. They had the same thought. *Could Agnes have unlocked the gate?*

Luke couldn't believe it. "Let's test it out."

He carried the crate to the gate. Right away, Agnes skipped over. She climbed on top and stretched her neck toward the lock. She slid the bolt, using her mouth. The gate swung open.

"Maaa! Maaa!" she called to the other animals. They filed behind her, and began to head out.

"Whoa! Wait!" Sarah pushed them back inside. Luke bolted the lock again.

"Well, that solves the mystery," he said. "And just in time." Grandma Rose and Grandpa Tom were driving up. And so was Dan.

"Everyone's back!" said Grandma Rose, smiling.

Grandpa Tom checked the animals carefully. "Nice work," he finally said.

The cousins told them everything— from rounding up the animals, to meeting Pete, to Snuffles having babies,

RUNNING AROUND

Goats are social. They hang out in groups and are friendly with people. They are smart too. And they really like to climb.

Farm Fact

UP IN A TREE

In Morocco, goats hang out in trees! They like to eat the tasty nuts and leaves of argan trees.

Groups of goats, called herds, have leaders and followers. They may bite and butt heads to work out which one will be the leader.

to Agnes opening the gate lock.

"How did you manage to do all this?" Grandpa asked, ruffling Luke's hair and tugging on Sarah's ponytail. The cousins beamed.

"Well, we've learned a lot these past few weeks," said Sarah.

"And today, we learned one more important thing," Luke added. Sarah groaned. It sounded like the lead up to a bad joke.

"To keep goats in the pen," Luke continued, "we need to move the lock to the *outside* of the gate!"

"And get that crate out of here too!" said Sarah.

Summer's End

The weeks passed quickly. Pete came to the farm every day. It turned out he and his parents had recently moved in down the road. It had been hard leaving his friends, Pete explained. And his older brother hadn't even been around. He'd been traveling with friends.

"Pete's like a little lost lamb," Sarah had told Luke. "We need to make him part of the farm."

So bit by bit, the cousins worked

with Pete. And bit by bit, Pete grew relaxed with the farm animals. He helped feed them. He helped groom them. By the end of the summer, he was doing chores on his own.

"See?" Luke joked. "That was our plan all along. To have you do all the work!"

Soon the nights grew cooler, the days shorter. Summer was ending. In no time, it was Luke's and Sarah's last day on the farm. Their grandparents prepared a farewell picnic lunch. Grandma Rose spread a blanket by the duck pond. Dan helped Grandpa Tom put out fresh fruits and vegetables. Pete and his parents came, bringing sandwiches and peanut butter twists.

After lunch, Luke stood up. "And now," he said in a deep announcer voice, "we have a special presentation." He pulled Sarah to her feet. They turned to Pete. "We talked to our grandparents. And our grandparents talked to your parents. And we all decided you should have—"

"An end-of-summer gift," Sarah announced. She lifted two baby bunnies from a carrying case.

"I thought that was another picnic basket!" Pete exclaimed. He grinned from ear to ear. "You mean these bunnies . . . Crackers! Crumbles! They're mine?"

"That's right, honey," Pete's mom said, smiling.

"We know you'll take good care of them," Grandpa Tom added.

· FARM BABIES ·

Baby animals are busy. Sometimes they hang out together. At other times they cuddle with their mom. And when they're ready, they take their first step, hop, or flight.

Puppies love to run, jump, and play. Then it's time for a long nap!

Baby geese, called goslings, practice using their wings before their feathers grow in.

Baby chicks can't fly until their wing feathers grow in. But they can jump!

Baby cows, called calves, have knobby knees and a wobbly walk.

Lambs talk to one another in bleats that sound like *baa* and *meh*.

A bed of straw in a quiet spot makes a perfect nest for a female barn cat and her kittens.

"You'd better!" said Luke. "We'll be back to check on them, you know."

"And that's why it's not so hard saying goodbye," said Sarah. "We'll all be together next summer."

Grandma Rose nodded. "There will be lots to do. We've decided to open a farm stand near the petting zoo."

"You'll be in charge of that too," Grandpa Tom said. "So get ready to work twice as hard."

Luke's and Sarah's parents came that afternoon. There were hugs, kisses, and some tears as they said goodbye to their grandparents. Then the cousins were on their way to vacation at the ocean cottage.

As soon as they arrived, it was time for the beach. Sarah got ready quickly. If they hurried, they could see the sunset. She waited impatiently for Luke. "What's taking so long?" she asked.

"I'm checking my list," Luke said. "Towels . . . camera . . . peanut butter twists . . ." The list went on and on.

"Why, Luke," Sarah teased, "you sound just like me. You have everything except the kitchen sink. Here!" She pretended to pull up the sink.

Luke laughed. "And you're joking around like me!" He grinned. "Only you're not as funny."

Just then a neighbor came to the door. He looked upset. "Have you seen a black-and-white cat?" he asked. "Ours ran away."

Luke and Sarah looked at each other. The beach could wait. They were ready to help!